DINER

THE SURGEON'S DILEMMA
Copyright © 2016 Brina Cary
Magic Wolf Publishing

e-book: 978-1-945409-06-6
Print: 978-1-945409-07-3

Printed in the USA.

Cover Design and Interior Format

WARDS OF AVALON

A MEDICAL ROMANCE

The SURGEON'S *Dilemma*

BRINA CARY

Acknowledgments

To Barbara Clark for the countless hours of live editing, breakfasts at Panera, for keeping me on task, and helping me to be a better author. Thank you!

To my very own immunologist, Dr. Hwang-Po, who has done her very best to help me live a healthier life. She has taught me about immune deficiency, patiently answered all of my questions, and reassured me whenever I need it. Thank you!

To the Killion Group for the beautiful cover, it truly is amazing, and to Jennifer Jakes for the wonderful formatting. It's always a lovely thing when I get the finished product and it makes all of the hours, weeks, and months of work worthwhile. Thank you!

Chapter 1

2004

DR. OLIVER BROOKS KNEW WHAT was coming. His stomach churned at the very thought of the conversation to come. Wiping his sweaty palms on his scrubs, he wished he could delay further, but the man deserved to know. His daughter was dead. Oliver had killed her.

Looking towards the waiting room he saw the patient's father, Nolan Woods, wringing his hands and glancing at the clock. It had been six hours since Oliver had last seen him, six hours since Oliver promised him that he'd see his daughter again soon. The confidence had been pride, pride that was his downfall. Little Lucy Woods was twelve years old. Twelve.

Oliver stood there — in the middle of the busy hallway — staring at Nolan Woods. People walked past him, jostling him as they went. The world moved around him. His feet would not move.

Past tense. Lucy Woods had been relegated to the past tense. She wouldn't have a future. There was nothing left for her. Nothing, but a funeral…

Dear God, how was he going to tell this man that his daughter was dead?

Oliver's lungs ached, burning from a lack of oxygen. He tried to take a deep breath, but he was too busy punishing himself. It was his fault.

"Get a hold of yourself," he whispered harshly. It wouldn't do for Mr. Woods to see him upset. The first rule of medical school was to never let it show. At least, that's what Oliver liked to believe. It wouldn't do to let her father see him so upset. Clearing his throat, determination gripped him. He would do this. He would do this for the little girl that loved unicorns, bright smiles, and sunny days.

"Mr. Woods," he called, his voice breaking. Taking a deep breath, Oliver schooled his features into what he hoped was a neutral look. Meanwhile, his soul was breaking into tiny pieces that could never be made whole again. There just wasn't enough glue.

Lucy's father turned towards him, hope evident in his eyes. He was about to destroy that hope.

Mr. Woods jumped up from the plastic looking couch and sped towards him. Oliver cringed at what was to come.

"Doc, how is she? I thought you said it would take a few more hours. I guess Lucy just did well. That's my girl." The smile on his face told Oliver that he was extremely proud of his little girl. She was the man's world after all...

"Mr. Woods, why don't we go in here to talk." He motioned to a room across the hall from the waiting room. It was more private, more intimate.

Mr. Woods didn't move, didn't blink, and his face took on a bright red tinge. "Whatever it is, please. Just tell me."

"Mr. Woods, let's go over here."

Oliver ushered him across the hall to the consultation room. It had a door that could close, allowing family members to grieve in private. Oliver hoped the low light would hide his face, should emotion begin to show. There was also a couch for family members and a chair directly across from it for doctors.

"I don't understand what's going on."

They sat. Oliver took a deep breath. He leaned forward and placed his elbows on his knees. It was no use trying to delay the inevitable any further, it was coming like a planned road construction, shutting off every avenue for escape. "Lucy…"

Oliver stopped, the man's face was rigid with concern. Eyes wide, he knew what was coming. Oliver just had to say the words to make them a reality. "There was a complication."

"Dear, God…" Oliver's heart broke for the man as his hands flew to his face. "She's ok though, right!?! Please say she's alright!"

Oliver sighed deeply, trying his damnedest to keep his throat from clogging, willing the sadness to go away. "All of the images that we did… Mr. Woods, we didn't catch a blood clot on the other side of the tumor. It didn't show."

Lucy's father sat on the couch that was reserved for these types of discussions. It was supposed to be soft and comforting, surrounded by the green paint on the walls. The overall effect was supposed to be calming. It never was.

The fear on his face made it worse. It was danger, raw danger, mixed with the desire to save his child. It was a look that Oliver had seen before… on his mother's face and every parent of every child he operated on.

The unicorn shirt caught his attention, drawing him back to Mr. Woods. Purples, blues, and reds all mixed together in the tail, forming a rainbow of colors around the unicorn. Unicorns were her favorite…

"Mr. Woods, when we began cutting the tumor away

the blood clot gave way. Your daughter… We couldn't save your daughter. I'm sorry. I'm truly sorry." There would never be a moment that he would ever forget this. It was his fault. Oliver should have known.

"This can't be right."

Oliver watched hopelessly as Lucy's father shook his head, denying the possibility that his daughter was dead. Emotions played out, quick to change on his Mr. Woods' face. Fear, anger, desperation, and finally… finally, rage.

"No. No, it's not right."

"I'm sorry, Mr. Woods." There were no other words. Nothing could fix it. Nothing change what had happened. Dear God, if only he could change it. If only there was a way for Oliver to go back in time, look at the images just one more time before doing the surgery. Maybe then he would have caught it… the clot that killed Lucy.

Lucy's father stood quickly and pointed an accusatory finger at Oliver. "This is your fault!" He began walking towards the door, but turned back. "How dare you! Lucy was scared and you told her it would be ok!" His breathing hiccuped, his eyes were red. Grief, raw grief reflected back at Oliver.

"You lied to my daughter and you lied to me… I didn't want to do this! I didn't want her to have the surgery this soon! This is your fault. I'm going to make sure you get what's coming to you!"

With hatred on his face, Mr. Woods walked back to Oliver. As the fist flew towards him, Oliver closed his eyes. It was only right to take it. The sound of flesh hitting flesh rang throughout the room. Connecting with the ground, Oliver's cheek burned. The man had a nasty right hook. Looking up, he saw Mr. Woods aim one last deadly look in his direction before storming out of the room.

Sitting on the dingy carpeted floor, Oliver knew he was

right. It was his fault. He should have known. There was always a chance that something could go wrong. If only Oliver had reviewed the scans himself, just one last time. Maybe then he would have seen it. Maybe then Lucy would be going into the Recovery Room instead of the Morgue. Maybe then Nolan Woods would still have his baby girl.

Chapter 2

2007

"OH, SHIT!" THE WORLD TILTED and the ground rushed up at him as he stumbled forward, shoes squeaking on the floor. Oliver managed to barely catch himself before going all the way down. It would have been a painful fall too, that ground was tile on top of concrete. No softness there. Looking to see what caused him to trip, Oliver realized he had stumbled over his own foot.

The feeling of falling was a scary thing, but to trip over one's own foot? Or feet?

His medical brain went full alert, automatically doing a run down for potential causes. His muscles ached, stress he surmised. His eyesight was blurry, too much caffeine he quipped. He couldn't remember the last time he ate... He froze, the conclusions he was left with weren't easy to accept. Of course he was human, but... was he exhausted?

As a neurosurgeon he had set hours, but now those set hours were frantic grasps of light sleep before going again. Between Avalon, where he was a surgeon, and here at the clinic, where he was the only physician, he had worked for hours and hours.

He continued his walk down the long hallway, overhead

fluorescent lights flickering. '*The ballast needs changing*', he reminded himself.

Working at the clinic wasn't the same as working at the hospital. It was real. It was all his responsibility, from the patients to the building maintenance. It put him right there with people. He actually had to speak with them, touch them, and evaluate them. There was no relying on scans and images. Or other people's findings. Working at the clinic with people that really needed him meant he had to find out what was wrong on his own terms.

It was different from Avalon, but it made him feel better. It made him feel like there was hope. Since Lucy Woods, there hadn't been much of that for him. He struggled to look in the mirror most days. He couldn't even remember the last time he did something fun. It wasn't his right. Lucy couldn't, why should he.

Clients couldn't pay, but it didn't matter. Helping was helping. Having red in his ledger drove him. Once it was black then he could let Lucy go. Not before.

Scrubbing at his neck, trying to wash away the hours of fatigue that ate away at him like a night that never ended, he hoped that it would be an easy day. They were never easy, but he could hope. It was the one thing he really had.

He took a deep breath and pasted a smile on his face. Looking at the bright pink clipboard on the door, he knew instantly that it was Synthia MacLemore's daughter. Once again.

'*Seriously? They've been in five times in the last month.*' Each time it was something different, but it was starting to make him nervous. It was like an itch he couldn't scratch, deep beneath the skin, cropping up randomly, making the bearer wonder if it was something benign or something to be wary of.

Synthia was a sweet young single mom, but Oliver suspected something was going on... Staring at the door with it's lime colored paint peeling away, Oliver's mind drifted.

The infections that Daniella had didn't make sense. According to Synthia, the child hadn't been around anyone that was ill. Yet, she constantly seemed to have a white blood cell count through the roof, fevers of a hundred and two, swollen lymph nodes, and negative lymphoma and leukemia tests. The whole thing was confusing the heck out of him. Only one possible cause remained... It was a heck of a leap too.

Oliver remembered his days as an intern in his very first few months. He spent one night in the ER... One. It still left a sour taste on his tongue, like the day old taste of whiskey gone sour.

Children should never be used as weapons in custody battles...

Could Synthia be doing the same thing? Oliver had never seen a husband before. However, people eluded him sometimes. If Synthia wasn't doing it, maybe someone else was?

The sound of laughter jarred him back to reality. While lost in his train of thought, he had opened the door without knocking. It was something unprofessional, something that would get him in serious trouble at Avalon. Glancing upon the scene that greeted him, it was worth the risk.

Synthia, unaware of his presence, was playing with Daniella. He had caught them in an unguarded moment. His lips curved up into a smile.

Synthia had paper cutouts of hearts attached to the lenses of her sunglasses and was making Daniella laugh. As he watched, Synthia pretended to be a movie star and Daniella pretended to be the paparazzi with her mother's outdated cell phone, taking pictures. They were at ease with each other, loving. Their faces both reflected peace. Laughter came from Daniella as Synthia smooched up her lips in a kiss and posed.

"Do it again, Mommy!" Daniella's delight spoke volumes to him. The childish voice was happy, a fresh welcome from his days of dealing with angry patients.

Oliver leaned against the doorframe in an easy manner, allowing it to support his stature. He wasn't a large man by any means, but he could be pretty imposing at six foot six. The image before him was one that he wanted to savor for as long as he could. It brought a feeling of warmth to his chest, a feeling that had been gone for far too long.

Oliver knew that Synthia wasn't capable of child abuse. There had to be something else going on. Either someone else was involved or there was something he was missing. He cleared his throat and watched amusedly as Synthia snatched the glasses off her face to hide her antics.

Slipping into doctor mode, he allowed her to pretend that he hadn't witnessed her unguarded moment. "Hi, Daniella. How are you feeling today?"

Daniella beamed a bright smile at him. The little girl's bright green eyes sparkled, reminding him of the ocean on a crisp day. "Mommy says I'm going to be all better soon."

"Did she now? Well, you know she's right. Mom's always are." He gave her a conspiratorial wink before turning to Synthia. It was important to get as much information as he could, he wouldn't miss something important again. "How are her symptoms?"

"It's the strangest thing." Synthia crossed her arms over her chest, as if warding off an attack. "Yesterday she was fine. Absolutely fine. Then this morning she woke up hoarse as can be. Her throat is white too. I'm worried that it might be strep, but there's no reason that it could be."

Her face was strained, her voice rough with concern. "She hasn't been around anyone with it!"

Another infection? "Daniella, do me a favor and open your mouth really wide for me." He grabbed the pen light from his jacket pocket and shined it in her throat. The back was encased with strep alright. He saw her two days ago though, it wasn't possible for it to have progressed this quickly…

"Daniella, can you do me a favor?" He did his best to keep the concern out of his voice, but it still wavered. She nodded happily. "Can you go get Nurse Beckett to swab your throat? Tell her that I said to give you two suckers when you're done."

Daniella hopped down from the little table and ran out of the room. The grape suckers were her favorite. Oliver was sure Nurse Beckett, the nurse that was working for pennies on the dollar, kept a whole bag of them just for Daniella.

Once the little girl was out of sight he leaned against the patient table. "Ms. MacLemore," he began.

"Synthia," she interrupted with an exaggerated tone.

He nodded absently. She had asked him to call her Synthia each time they had discussed Daniella's symptoms — her condition. He just felt odd about it, it was such a taboo thing to do… It felt as if it was leading to dangerous things… "Synthia, Daniella didn't have strep when you brought her in two days ago."

"Could it have just been hiding and causing all of this?"

He shook his head, there was no chance. Well, there was a chance… in a place called Hell that wasn't ever going to freeze over. "I'm afraid not. I'm concerned that something else might be going on." With strep, Oliver knew that Daniella wasn't being harmed by someone else. It wasn't something easy that he could fix either. He needed help. He needed Jack's help.

"I think something might be wrong with her immune system." He crossed his arms over his chest. "It's weird to come on now without showing signs before. Normally, things like this show signs early. Was she this sick when she was younger?" If she had been, he could find a way to fix the problem before it got worse, before there was a possibility of… Dani taking the same path as Lucy.

Life couldn't be that unfair, but Oliver knew it could be. Oliver knew better than anyone that life was a fickle bitch, the bully in the playground that stole your lunch money, the co-worker that passed your work off as their own, the blood clot that lay under a tumor…

"How early?" Synthia wrung her hands and shifted from foot to foot.

He mentally shook himself. It was important to put Lucy aside. This was Daniella. Daniella wasn't Lucy. "She would have shown signs within hours of being born… severe illness. Did she?"

"No, she was always well as a baby. She never got sick, not until a few months ago."

"I would like to talk to a friend at a local hospital about your daughter's symptoms. He's a really good guy and he's one of the best in his field. Are you ok with that?" Oliver watched her face for signs that she might resist. If she did, he'd still talk to Jack. He just wouldn't tell her. As long as he didn't use names or provide her medical information, and just kept it all hypothetical, then he would be alright — or at least, that's what he would keep telling himself.

"Is it serious?"

"I honestly don't know. My friend is an immunologist and can give me a better idea of how to help your daughter."

Her head tilted to the right just a smidge. Her mouth

tightened. She was processing it, categorizing it, and form-ing a response. Oliver had seen the same look a hundred times. It was a process that needed to happen, one that he wouldn't hinder by words. She would speak when ready.

"A better idea…? An immunologist?" The words were drawn out. Hope that she was misinterpreting him. He recognized that too. Years of being a doctor told him when a patient was hearing words that they didn't want to hear — words they wished they weren't hearing.

"He helps people with immune issues." Oliver didn't know how to soften the blow. There wasn't much he could do other than be up front with her.

"Doc, I'm not an idiot. I know what an immunologist is. I just don't understand why Dani needs one. I've never been ill, not a day in my life. Did I do something wrong? Did I not do something that I should have?"

The fear on her face took Oliver by surprise. It was something that he wasn't prepared for, even after all of the cases he saw every day, he wasn't prepared for the fear. It made his chest ache. Absently, he tried to rub the aching feeling away.

"Honestly, I don't know that there's an issue. She could just be at that age where most kids are germ factories. They could turn a cough into a plague." He tried to smile to put her at ease, but she seemed to ignore him. Oliver cleared his throat. "Let me talk to him and I'll get back with you. In the meantime, here is my personal cell. You call me if anything happens. I don't care what time it is. Ok?" He handed her the card and she took it without a fight. That act told Oliver a lot. Synthia was a proud woman, he had learned that over the last few months that she'd been bringing Daniella to see him. For her to eagerly accept his help, Oliver now knew that she would do whatever was needed to help her daughter. That could very well save her daughter's life if what he suspected turned out to be the case.

Chapter 3

*K*NOCK. JACK IGNORED HIM. *KNOCK.* Jack still ignored him. *Knock.* On the third knock to the wooden frame, Oliver watched with glee as Jack's shoulders hunched. He had him and he knew it. Jack couldn't ignore the third time, never could.

The answering sigh was Jack's way of saying that he hoped the interruption at his door was quick. Oliver laughed at his friend's antics. "Hey, Jack," he greeted warmly.

Stepping in the room, he surveyed it quickly. Nothing had changed since the last time he'd been there. Superhero paraphernalia, in the form of action figures, were lined in a haphazard way on Jack's desk. There had been a battle between them, several taking refuge under stacks of paper that had probably once been in an orderly pile.

His mug that promised to protect the multiverse was next to the edge with what looked like day old coffee as it's forgotten contents. Jack wasn't a slob, he was just busy — too focused to remember that fresh coffee was available hourly from the lounge.

"Oliver!" Jack jumped up from his desk and Oliver entered the room. "Hey! How's everything going? It's been forever since I've seen you."

They both went quiet. It had been a while, but they both knew why. Oliver had pulled back from everyone after Lucy's death.

Oliver cleared his throat and stared down at the dirty red carpet. It had been close to ten years since it had been replaced. The hospital had offered new carpet twice, but Jack had refused both times. Oliver took a deep breath. "Jack, I've got a favor that I need to ask you."

"Anything. Just name it."

Jack was serious too. Oliver felt like a heel for avoiding him as much as he had. It had just been hard to do anything else. "I need this to stay a secret. It can't leave these walls."

Jack motioned for them to sit in the chairs in front of his desk. Upon sitting, they turned the chairs towards each other. "Oliver, are you in trouble?"

"What?" What kind of question was that? He shook his head, "No, it's nothing like that." He took a deep breath. He was about to tell someone, for the first time, just what he was doing outside of the hospital. "Jack, there's a reason I've been so anti-people." He sighed deeply. "I started a non-profit clinic after… When I'm not here, I'm there."

"What?" Shock, fear, and concern laced his words. Jack couldn't believe what he was hearing, Oliver couldn't believe it had taken him so long to tell him about his crime.

Oliver knew just how bad it looked. He had broken the rules. He had broken them to atone for Lucy.

"Man, do you realize just how much trouble you could be in if they found out?"

"Yes, that's why I didn't tell anyone. I see patients there, as a primary care doctor."

"So, from neurosurgeon to primary care doctor?"

"Yep."

"You realize that's kind of like going from Bruce Wayne to Batman everyday, right?"

"So do you want to be Commissioner Gordon or not?" He had to speak Jack's language. That's the only way he could get him to agree to help.

"Oh, I'm totally in. You know how big of a geek I am. What do you need?"

"I have a patient. She's five years old, but keeps getting recurrent infections. Her latest is strep throat. Two days before I saw her for that, her throat was fine. There was no evidence of strep. None. Then when I saw her again with the strep… Her throat looked like it had gone untreated for over a week. Her white blood cell count was nineteen."

"Nineteen thousand?"

He nodded, "An hour later it was twenty-two. In the last month there's been a handful of other infections too. Things that just don't make sense. I keep thinking about the ER… the Sanders case. Normally without there being a history of immune issues in the family, this could possibly signal something like child abuse, but the mom is a sweetheart. She loves the kid and no one else is harming her…"

"So, what are you thinking?"

The look on Jack's face told Ollie that the question was rhetorical; he took a deep breath to answer anyway. "I'm thinking something is wrong with her immune system, but I can only do so many blood tests at the clinic. We just don't have the equipment."

"Are you asking me to break protocol?"

"I'm simply asking for your help." If that meant breaking protocol then that too.

"Fine. I have a study going on right now that's looking at immune deficiencies in children. I'm going to give you six tubes. I need them filled at least a fourth of the way full and given back to me. I can say they're for research, as long as the mom agrees."

Oliver knew just how big of a risk Jack was taking for him. If the Research Compliance Officer found out… "Thank you."

"Oh, I'm going to ask you for a favor in the future and you're going to do it, no questions asked. Got it, Batman?"

He understood and he would do it. Jack was helping him to keep a child alive. There wasn't much that he wouldn't do in exchange. "Jack, I really appreciate…"

"Don't worry about it. Just remember that you owe me. Now about the samples, I need them as soon as they're taken."

"Traffic is about fifteen minutes."

"Pack them in a cooler with dry ice. Give them only to me."

"I'll have them for you tomorrow morning. I can get Synthia to bring her in on her way to school."

"Good. It'll take about a week to get the results back. I'll let you know as soon as I have them."

"Jack…"

"I said don't worry about it. Just know that the favor I ask is going to be payment enough." The grin Jack flashed Oliver told him all that he needed to know. It was going to involve some serious entertainment on Jack's part. They had been friend's since their college freshmen days, going through medical school together. They knew everything there was to know about each other. Heck, Oliver had even taken Jack out to the bar on occasion to forget about his latest conquest that broke up with him.

Jack was a great friend, but that's as far as it went. He knew that Jack wanted more, but he just wasn't drawn to him in a romantic way. He hoped one day that Jack found a great guy that was though.

The guy had been through a lot in college. It took six weeks before Oliver realized that the reason Jack never spoke was because he thought Oliver hated him because he was gay. The look on his face when Oliver had told him that he didn't care as long as he didn't bring anyone over when it was exam time… He didn't think he'd ever forget it. Jack had looked so relieved. They'd been friends since.

"Don't forget. First thing in the morning. I'll have to get Ada to mail it out to our external lab for testing. It could just be a regular immune deficiency, but normally those crop up before five years old." Oliver felt hope being crushed at Jack's next words. "It could be something worse. Something that's more your department than mine. You need to be prepared for that."

"Whatever." Turning on his heel, he hoped that Jack hadn't heard the waver in his voice. It was there, like he was a child all over again, mourning his mother. It was important to be confident. Confidence was paramount. *Slow breaths. You can do it.* He took a step toward the door. Jack's laughter stopped him. It was low, demeaning, and self-depreciating. "What?"

"I just realized that this is why you quit hanging out." His voice was sad, regretful. The tone of a man that realized he hadn't tried hard enough.

Was this fixable? Or had he lost his best friend? There just weren't enough hours in the day when one was trying to hide regret. Ironically, it brought about greater regret. "I didn't want to tell you because then you wouldn't have plausible deniability."

"Plausible deniability? Ollie, you've been watching way too many cop shows."

"We've all got to start somewhere."

"And, that ride in the backseat of that cop car at twenty one wasn't enough for you?"

"What was that for again?"

"Punching that frat kid in the face." The smile on Jack's face told Oliver that he remembered it fondly. The guy had been hassling Jack for weeks. Destroying his belongings, mentioning him in rude ways... inappropriate ways.

"Yeah, sorry that it took me so long to do it."

"You were busy." Jack shrugged it off, like it was no big deal, but to Oliver... it was. It was just another failure, once again something that he should have done differently in life. It had been made right though. Well, as right as he could make it.

"I shouldn't have been." Oliver felt as if a truck had run him down on a backroad going ninety miles an hour, with a haul of cattle. Jack had always been there for him, even now.

"Oliver, we all make mistakes. We all get busy. Just don't forget that you still owe me a favor." Jack's voice was tired, worn out. His words were smooth like a day old pond, but there was an underlying message. Jack had forgiven him.

Chapter 4

OLIVER LAY IN HIS KING sized bed looking at the skylights above. The night's sky was clear and for once he could see the stars above. As a child he had been given just about anything he could have ever wanted, except time with his family. His mother died when he was nine and his father couldn't be bothered with him.

The required parent visits to his boarding schools, the occasional Christmas card, etc was all the time his father spent with him. The boarding schools had served him well though. Oliver hadn't even needed a single dime from his father to pay for college or med school, but that didn't stop the man from bragging about his successful neuro-surgeon son — the one he didn't raise.

A deep sigh helped clear his thoughts. Looking over at the clock on his nightstand he confirmed that he had to be up in three hours. He could either lay in bed and hope to get an hour of sleep or begin preparing for his day. He had two surgeries at the hospital, that he had already worked around his time at the clinic. He also had to get Daniella's blood. Synthia was scheduled to bring her by at seven thirty.

A shrill beep from his phone interrupted his thoughts. Who would be calling him at this hour? He hoped it wasn't an emergency case. Those were awful. The last one he attended was a kid that had crashed his motorcycle. Nineteen years old and the kid had destroyed four vertebrae and fractured his skull.

"Dr. Brooks," he answered.

"Oh my god! Thank God you answered!"

"Synthia?"

"It's Dani! Oh God! Oh God! I don't know what's wrong! Oh my God, I don't know what to do! She's running a fever of a hundred and three and she can't speak! My baby was fine this afternoon! She was fine! She said her head was hurting, but I figured it was the strep! I don't know what to do!"

He was already out of bed and searching for a pair of jeans. "Synthia, you have to calm down. Have you called an ambulance?"

"They won't come here! We live in… in a bad part of town."

She sounded so hesitant that Oliver wondered where she could possibly live that would make her so reluctant to tell him. "Tell me where you live and I'll come get you." Now that he thought about it he had never asked where his patient's lived. He had assumed that they lived around the clinic, near enough to use it's services. What if some lived further away than he thought? Did they travel miles to get to the clinic?

"We live in… the gas lamp district."

Oliver could hear the utter shame in her voice. The gas lamp district was where druggies and hookers lived. It was also thirty minutes from the clinic. She was right, ambulances didn't go to that area at night. At least, they didn't without police presence. It was too dangerous. They had no business living there.

"Synthia," he said in his best doctor voice, "I'm leaving

now. It'll take me about ten minutes to get there. Wrap her in a blanket and try to get her to talk to you, try to keep her awake. I'll honk when I get there. Don't come outside until then."

"Please hurry! I'm so scared!"

"I'm going to stay on the phone with you, it's going to be ok. Just keep talking to her. Tell her a story if you need to. It's going to be ok. I'm on my way." He grabbed the keys to his jeep, slipped his shoes on his feet, and ran out the door. He listened intently as her tearful voice filled the line, listening for anything that might give a hint to a change in Daniella's condition.

He would make it in seven minutes if he ran a few lights. If the cops pulled him over then he would explain that he was tending to a medical emergency. They wouldn't follow him into the gas lamp district anyway.

Chapter 5

THE WALLS IN THE SMALL waiting room were an eerie color late at night. It was a mix of blue and gray, a color that signified illness. The lights were dimmed because of the late hour, but people still wandered about. A nearby man looked out the window into the darkness, muttering about it taking forever. A nearby elderly woman knitted as she awaited word on her husband who had tumbled over a rug and had a nasty bruise.

He hoped no one recognized him, but it was the closest hospital — Avalon, where he worked… If they did, he only hoped that Synthia didn't tell them how they knew each other. None of them knew about the clinic.

Taking a deep calming breath, he studied the scuffed tile floor. There was a strange pattern of black marks next to one window, as if purposefully left by a shoe repeatedly striking.

He'd lose it all if she did tell them. He'd lose everything he had worked for, since his first night in boarding school.

"Synthia, don't worry. Everything is going to be alright."

"How do you know that?" Her voice broke as she screamed the question at him. Her face was flushed and pale, her eyes wide and bright. Fear reflected back at him.

Oliver took another deep, calming breath. He was a surgeon, he dealt with terrible moments in people's lives. He could handle this…

Shit… who was he kidding. This was a mama bear on a rampage, frightened for her little girl. There was no way he could tell her it was ok, especially when he didn't have a clue. Closing and opening his mouth didn't help to get the words to form. He couldn't lie to her.

Leaning back in the hard chair, he decided to throw the truth out there to her. She deserved to know. "Honestly, I don't know that. I've been on the other side of the fence and I work with these guys. I trust them. I know they'll do everything they can to help her."

"Oh, really? I suppose that makes everything just hunky dory. Just because you're a doctor doesn't mean you know these guys. Or do all of you doctors get together and play pool on weekends?" She was being sarcastic and for some reason it brought a grin to his face. Her daughter was in a place that she couldn't go, which was terrifying her, and she still showed her personality.

She glared at him like he was a gallon of spoiled milk. "Quit smiling at me. I have no idea what's going on and it's making me angry. I also don't know how I can pay for this. I told you to take us to Saint Luke's. They'll work with me on the payments."

Tilting his head sideways he wondered about her words. Her voice lacked anger, but held a tinge of worry. She was worried about the money, he surmised. However, it seemed like there was also a bit of sadness surrounding "Saint Luke's". The way it rolled off her tongue, the finality, struck him as odd.

"Saint Luke's wouldn't be able to help her. These guys can." He carefully considered his next words like they were the executioner's chance at condemnation. They could be too. "There's something that I need to tell you though… please don't get upset…"

"Why would I get upset? What would possibly upset me?"

Oliver watched as she stood up from the hard plastic green chair, clenching at her jeans until her hands turned white. He vaguely wondered if his mother had ever been this worried about him… before she… He sighed deeply, to dispel the thoughts that were beginning to form. It wasn't possible for him to handle that right now. *Synthia, focus on Synthia.*

"Synthia,I work here. These are my guys. I'm a neuro-surgeon here, I work at the clinic in my free time."

He watched her take a step back and narrowed her eyes at him. Her brow furrowed, her lips thinned. He waited with baited breath for whatever she was about to say, expecting the worst.

"You must be a terrible surgeon then."

"Come again?" Whatever remark he had expected, he certainly hadn't expected that. The words shocked him, an icy bath on a hot summer's day.

"You're always at the clinic. That means you either do surgeries at night or you rarely do surgeries. If you rarely do them then you must be bad at it."

A deep laugh escaped him. She was one feisty woman. "No, I schedule my surgeries around my time at the clinic. The clinic is open Tuesday, Thursday, Saturday, and Sunday. I do my surgeries the other days. It can make for some long days, but the clinic is needed." Speaking of… "Synthia, you can't tell anyone about the clinic here. They don't know. I could get in a lot of trouble if they found out."

"What do you want me to say then?" She crossed her arms over her chest, like she was daring him to ask her to lie.

"I honestly don't know. They'll call you back any minute. It's up to you, I'm not going to ask you to lie. I just need you to know that the clinic could get shut down if they find out about it."

"I still don't understand why I had to wait out here! She's a child for God's sake! She needs her mother!"

"Because she was in immediate need of care. Trust them."

The door opened and a nurse called Synthia's name. Oliver sat back in the waiting room chair while she went to talk to the nurse. It was Rena, she knew him. His whole career was about to come crashing down. Rena would tell half the hospital before the end of her shift. If that happened then the board would force him to close the clinic and reprimand him… possibly report him. There was no way they would leave it and just ignore that he was violating his contract with them.

A few minutes later the door opened again. Rena came out and stood in front of him. He was waiting for the recriminating look, but she was smiling. It was a gentle happy smile too. "Rena?"

"Oh! You should have told us! You can bet that half the hospital will know by morning. Mac's already sending emails."

Synthia had told them everything… His shoulders slumped, he was doomed. There'd be no way he could make up for Lucy now.

"You sly dog."

What? His head shot up. What exactly had she told them to make Rena say that? Had Synthia told them something else? "Told you what?" His stomach clenched.

"That you were engaged, silly." She grabbed his forearm and pulled him up out of the chair. "I can't believe you're sitting out here while they're back there. Don't you worry either. We've got the little one in a great room and we have a specialist coming to look at her too. We're going to take great care of your soon to be family. Your family is our family."

As she hauled him through the door, he felt panic assault him from all sides. She had kept his secret, but instead told everyone they were getting married...

What in the world was he going to do? He couldn't be a husband! He couldn't even remember where he parked his car after a busy day!

Rena stopped, examining him, fear and confusion reflected in her gaze. "Are you hyperventilating?"

He shook his head and tried to get himself under control. Synthia may have told them that, but that didn't mean it had to happen. No, there wasn't anything that said he had to marry her.

"You ok?"

"Yes, I'm ok." In reality he was far from it, but it wouldn't do to tell Rena that.

"Good. Now come on, they're waiting for you."

"Who?"

"You're family."

The words caused the ground to rush up to him as colors blurred, his stomach dropped, and a heat blazed through his core.

He was passing out.

"Dr. Brooks!"

His knees took the shock as he fell to them, his head pounding. *A family?* He couldn't have a family. There was no way, not with how he had been raised. He didn't know the first thing about having a family other than what a funeral looked like. That wasn't something one forgot at such a young age either.

"Dr. Brooks, you have to calm down. Breathe."

Rena's cold hands on his face brought him back to reality. There was no family for him. Just a woman trying to save her kid. Just a father that abandoned him. Just a mother that died.

Chapter 6

JACK? THEY CALLED JACK? OF all the people they could have called... they called Jack.

Oliver looked at his friend with sadness. If they called Jack then it had to be bad. They wouldn't have called him at three a.m. unless it was really bad, unless Synthia was going to have to make some hard choices.

Resisting the urge to reach for her, to comfort her, was hard. It was like fighting the urge to get coffee in the morning. One knew that without the dark, ebony colored elixir of happiness nothing would get done. Yet, one always tried to resist. It was strange... feeling like that with her. She was a patient's mother. Nothing else.

Yeah, keep telling yourself that, a small voice within whispered.

"Hey, Ollie," Jack greeted before looking over towards Synthia who sat in the chair next to Daniella's bed. "You must be Synthia, Oliver's fiancee." Jack winked at Synthia. "I'm Jack, his best bud."

Damn. Even he had heard about it. Oliver was sunk now. There was no safe exit from this situation. He glared at Synthia, and she grinned in return. Her hair fanned her face and her eyes seemed to be full of mirth, judging from the way the tiny laugh lines crinkled. He was in so much trouble.

"Hi, Jack. Wish we could have met under better circumstances…" Her voice trailed off. The worry was back.

"Oh, don't give it a second thought." Jack waved her words away, like he didn't understand she was talking about Daniella. Oliver wanted to flick him in the forehead but knew Jack better than that. He was trying to be comforting and remove her concern.

"Oliver doesn't know it yet, but I'm going to be the best man."

Oliver decided that the first chance he got he was going to flick him in the forehead…

They were talking about him like he wasn't even present. "Jack," he growled in warning.

Jack winked at Synthia before turning to Oliver. "Is this the little one you were going to get me blood samples for?"

"Yes, but something came up." It happened so fast too, faster than Ollie had ever seen. Maybe Jack was used to little kids getting sick within hours, but he wasn't.

"This will be easier. We can run all the tests we need now."

Synthia sat up straight and Oliver knew what was coming. "I can't pay for this!"

Jack's confused look made Oliver feel guilty. No, he hadn't told her. They weren't really engaged. Well, technically they were, he just hadn't been the one to ask. In fact, he hadn't asked or been asked at all.

"Ollie didn't tell you?"

"Tell me what?"

"Once you get married you get his health insurance coverage. As a hospital employee, anything done here is covered. It's a benefit."

"Does it cover us while engaged?"

Oliver had a feeling that she would stay engaged forever if that were the case, not that he could blame her. He could see the hope on her face. Unfortunately, he was about to break her heart. Sighing deeply he whispered, "Only married couples." He focused back on Jack. "What did the initial tests show?"

"Her white blood cell count is at twenty-seven now. Her platelet count is dropping. They started her on I.V. antibiotics… She's septic."

Septic? How could she possibly be septic? Septicemia takes days, weeks… not hours. "From what?"

A thousand different things ran through his mind. Things he could have missed. Pneumonia, being the worst. *Had she coughed? Was her breathing coming from her stomach or her chest? Had she given him any sort of sign?*

"Oliver, you didn't miss anything, so quit thinking that. We don't know what's going on right now. We don't know what's causing this. It could be anything or nothing. The cultures won't be back for a few days, so we just need to wait and try to treat her symptoms the best we can."

"Take a guess."

"I'm thinking that her immune system is failing her because of something that's attacking her body. I don't think this is a normal immune deficiency though." He went silent and Oliver's stomach flipped. "Ollie, I'm requesting an MRI to go with the blood cultures."

Jack was trying to tell him that this was serious. More serious than he was prepared to tell Synthia. "Jack, are you thinking Montoya's field or mine?"

"Montoya's," the flat answer resonated around the room. The skin on his arms and the back of his neck raised up, giving him chills. His heart skipped a beat, then beat three times in the space of one.

Montoya was a pediatric oncologist.

Oliver tried to find his voice, but it was hard. Synthia looked back and forth between them. How was he going to tell her? How was he going to be the one to break her heart? How was he going to be the one to destroy the hope in her eyes?

"Someone please tell me who Montoya is? Please?" Her face was frantic. Her golden brown eyes drilled into his soul, breaking it into a thousand pieces before gluing it back together again. "Oliver?"

There was no way that he was going to risk Daniella being sent to Saint Luke's. No way...

"We're going to go get married right now." The words came out more forcefully than he intended, but they were true. He would have to deal with his fears later, the stomach dropping worry of failure and loss that assaulted him at the thought of commitment. If he needed to do that — marriage — for her then he would.

Montoya was a bit of a bastard. A great doctor, but a bastard. He would send her to Saint Luke's... Daniella would die, unless he forced Montoya to take her case.

"Married? Seriously, married?"

He stood up and walked to her. He grabbed her by her forearms, "Synthia, just trust me." Tears were gathering in her eyes. "Do you trust me?" She nodded and he smiled sadly at her. Oliver knew that she understood something was wrong and that he was trying his best to fix it. "We're going to get married right now."

"I can't leave her here. What if she wakes up?" She cast a look upon her sleeping daughter. Daniella was so tiny, taking up such a small space on the large bed.

A cough from Jack interrupted Oliver's reply. Looking toward Jack, he knew that his friend would be the voice of sanity in this hair brained scheme. He would be the voice that walked Ollie through everything that needed to be done. The man knew what it meant to him, to take this chance. "The Chaplain will do it for you. He'd love to do a wedding."

Frank certainly would love to do a wedding. Frank loved weddings. Unfortunately, Oliver would have to tell him the truth — would have to tell him that he was biting the bullet of fear because of Lucy. There was no way he was going to let another child die, not when there was something that he could do about it.

A tiny thought began to tweak his conscience, a thought of who Frank might tell... The air whooshed out from his lungs, as if he had been sucker punched in the stomach. The lights danced before his eyes.

Once Oliver told Frank what was going on... Frank would call his father. The men had been friends since Oliver was five. There's no way that Frank would keep that secret. His father would know... His father would know that Ollie was creating a family.

Chapter 7

"FRANK, WE NEED TO TALK." Oliver cringed at the ominous tone in his voice. Frank was going to think he was dying if he kept that up. He needed to keep his voice light and airy. That was the only way Frank could possibly believe the load of BS that Ollie was about to serve him...

However, as Frank looked up from his desk, Oliver felt his heart break. There was no way he could lie to him. If you discounted the whole going-to-Hell-for-lying-to-a-man-of-the-cloth thing, then you had to take into account that Frank never faltered. The man was a rock, not gypsum either. The man was granite. He stood behind you, defending you no matter what, even if you broke a forty thousand dollar vase playing baseball in the country club.

He was going to have to tell Frank the full truth, even if it meant a call to his father.

"Hey, Ollie. It's awfully early for you," he said as he looked at his watch, concern dripping from his words.

Checking his own watch, Ollie realized that it was just after five in the morning. "Yeah, there's something important that I need to talk to you about."

The look went from slight concern to the look of a

Chaplain waiting for the other foot to drop as Frank motioned to a chair. Oliver took it. Brushing a hand through his hair, he sighed deeply. There was no easy way to say it. "Frank, I'm getting married."

"I'm sorry. Do what?" Frank sat completely still with one eyebrow raised, the other lowered. He then began to slowly look around the room.

"What are you looking for?"

"A camera, this IS a joke, right? Did Leia put you up to this?"

A sad laugh escaped him. "No, your wife didn't put me up to this. You heard me right, I'm getting married. I want you to do the ceremony, but her daughter is really sick. She's here and they're going to send her to Saint Luke's if we don't get married ASAP."

Frank's shoulders eased and the Chaplain within took over, he understood. "What's wrong?"

"They don't know, but Jack thinks it's cancer."

"Who will be handling the case here?"

"Montoya…" Oliver knew that would be all he needed to say. "Montoya is being called in…"

"That man won't see her?"

Oliver shook his head. "No insurance. You know the policy."

"Saint Luke's can't handle that. They do great at little things, but pediatric cancer… that's a whole other ballgame and a half."

"I know. That's why we need to get married ASAP." It hurt to say those words. He never wanted to get married. He never wanted to share his life with anyone.

Frank sighed a deep, weary sigh and Oliver could tell he had already thought up a plan. "Well, Montoya comes in at nine. City Hall opens at eight. Can you get over there and get the license right away? If so, then we can have you guys married before Montoya has a chance to turn them away. I can also keep him a bit busy until Stacy in HR, has a chance to process the paperwork. She's a good gem, won't take her long at all."

The drive from City Hall was ten minutes. A wedding could be done in five. HR… HR would take thirty minutes, didn't matter if Frank thought it wouldn't take them long or not. If Frank could keep Montoya busy for a bit, then maybe he could do it. "We need someone to stay with Daniella until we return."

"Don't worry about it." Frank's smile made him wonder what tricks he had planned. "Ollie, I've got that covered. Let's go get your bride and make sure you have all the documents City Hall will ask for. Normally there's a waiting period, but tell Denis he owes me a favor. He'll get it done for you. I'll make sure he's there."

Frank's word was better than Hammurabi's Law. He didn't break it unless he was forced to. If he was forced to, it didn't end well. Ollie could count on him, even if he couldn't count on anyone else.

Chapter 8

OLIVER WATCHED HELPLESSLY AS SYNTHIA slid on the freshly cleaned floor, racing into Daniella's room, grimacing as he himself lost his footing. Sliding to the left, he realized he was going down. The ground rushed up at him and he turned toward his side.

They had been delayed at City Hall. They had fifteen minutes to get married and get HR to process their wedding certificate. Fifteen minutes…

"At least the baseball games were good for something."

That voice… Dread creeped into every inch of Ollie's body, wringing his heart and causing a crescendo of beats, much like Bethoveen's Ninth, between his ears. He closed his eyes and prayed to any Holy being that might grant him a favor that it wasn't true. He wished upon any star that might be in the morning's sky that the owner of that voice wasn't really standing a few feet from him.

It couldn't be him. It just couldn't.

Why would he be here? There was no reason for him to be here.

Looking up, Ollie saw that the man he dreaded seeing, out of everyone in the entire world, was there. The man that he couldn't stand being in a room with, ever since he was ten, was there. The man was holding onto Synthia and smiling at him.

Oliver's mouth opened and closed. For some reason his voice box wouldn't work. Shock? Maybe.

"Seeing as how he's too dumbstruck to introduce us, I'm Drake Brooks. I'm Ollie's dad."

"Oh! I'm Synthia, Oliver's…" She went blank and looked to Ollie.

Oliver stood up, trying to brush off the anger that threatened to emerge. "Fiancee," he provided as calmly as he could.

"I figured that much." His father smirked.

Ollie frowned. Drake Brooks was a lot of things in Ollie's book, but he wasn't a moron. He would have picked Synthia out right away, even if they hadn't come rushing in together.

"Frank called you." It was an accusation. Judging from the look on Frank's face, it fit perfectly. It wasn't a surprise that Frank called, after all he had expected it, but it certainly was a surprise that he showed. What had Frank told his father?

It didn't matter. They were short on time. "Frank, we're running out of time here. We need to get this done quickly."

"He told me why we're on a time limit, but when there's more time there's going to be a proper wedding." His father spoke as if his words were law. Ignoring him was going to be hard, but Ollie had to try. As his father turned away from him and toward Frank, Ollie remembered why it had been twelve years since they had more than a two minute phone conversation…

It was like he was being shut out once again. Told that he needed to do better, to be better. The same thing his father had been telling him, without words, since his mother died.

"Frank, since we're in such a big hurry, let's get started." His father motioned for Frank to carry on and went to stand by Daniella's bed.

"Ollie, do you take Synthia?" Frank's eyes reminded Ollie of a game of hockey, ricocheting between Synthia and himself, waiting for answers.

A feeling as if his breath wouldn't come stole over Ollie. Could he really do this? It's not like it would be permanent. Just to get Daniella the treatment she needed. He could do that. He could pretend it was alright, just for a bit.

"Yes." The word was a whisper, echoing around the room. The meaning slammed into him, rocking his soul. He was marrying a woman he hardly knew. He was marrying a woman that needed more than he could give.

"Synthia, do you take Ollie, even though he's being a prick?" Frank's crude words elicited a giggle from her. It was a child-like laugh, full of promise and love. It made him ache to hear it again.

It was the first time he had heard her laugh, when it wasn't Daniella bringing it out of her. Of course, there hadn't been much to laugh about when she and Ollie had talked. They always talked about Daniella's health.

"I guess so," she said with a smile.

"Then you two are married. Don't worry, we'll do it proper next time. For now, it'll do."

"Great! Sign the paper, so I can get it to Stacy." Two minutes. That's all he had left.

"Oh, that's already done."

"What?" Oliver turned toward him, anger rolling just beneath the surface.

"Yeah, that's why I said to see Denis. He faxed it over earlier. I've already signed it and given it to Stacy. She's already updated your W-7 form to show you're married to Synthia. You should have a copy of the paperwork any minute."

"Are you serious?" He couldn't be serious. It had to be a joke. There was no way that Frank had done that when they were racing to get it all done before Montoya showed. No way.

"Yes, why wouldn't I be?" The look of innocence was a farce, of that Ollie was sure. Unless Frank was secretly a diabolical man that derived pleasure in torturing innocent people…

Oliver threw his hands up in the air. "We nearly killed ourselves trying to get back in time and you had already signed the paper and submitted it!" He was a dead man. It didn't matter that he was a Chaplain. Oliver was going to kill him and make it look like an accident. Or maim him. Being a neurosurgeon did have it's advantages. He new exactly where all the nerves were.

"Oliver, it's ok. We're here and it's done. Please, don't do this in front of Daniella." Synthia's words were strained as they pleaded with him.

Daniella. The little girl who was now his daughter. Turning to look at her, he regretted his behavior. She was so pale, almost blending into the crisp white sheets on the hospital bed.

"Hey, sleepyhead", he whispered at her as he walked to her bedside.

"Are you fighting?"

He sat in the chair next to the bed, pulling it closer to her, and leaned forward. He smoothed back her curly blond hair and smiled. "No, sweetie. We were just talking loudly. Grownups do that sometimes."

"Before daddy died, him and mommy fighted a lot." Her eyes were focused on the stuffed blue teddy bear sitting on the counter across the room. It was just one of a few toys that had mysteriously shown up since Ollie's engagement had been announced through the Gossip Line at Avalon.

"It's fought and how do you know that, sweetheart?" He could hear the quiver in her voice.

Synthia had no clue that her little girl knew about the arguments. She had no idea that little ears could hear and remember all of the harsh words parents say when they're angry.

"I heard you."

He got up and sat on the bed beside Daniella, blocking her view of her mother. "Sweetie, I'm going to let you in on a secret. Parents sometimes get really mad at each other. They sometimes say mean things because they're upset. They don't mean any of them and then feel really bad about it. Have you ever said something mean to someone?"

"Yeah, Charlie."

He hid his grin, and the laugh that threatened to erupt, by biting his lip. Charlie was the clinic's pet goldfish, the one Daniella confided secrets in. "How did it make you feel?"

"It made him cry. I cried too."

"See that's what happens when parents say mean things to each other."

"Do you feel bad?"

The curious question hit him in the gut. "I feel bad about a lot of things," he whispered, his voice breaking from emotion. Lucy Woods being the foremost of those things.

"Then I think you should kiss and make up."

His father's boisterous laugh echoed off the walls. "I think that's a great idea!"

Oliver glared at him. Unfortunately, his hope of his

glare causing his father to spontaneously combust was not to be. "This isn't the time nor the place."

"Oh, on the contrary, it's actually the perfect time and place. You just got married. You need to kiss the bride. My little granddaughter is the brightest here." His father winked at Daniella, two conspirators in the making.

Fine, if it would get them to stop, he would kiss Synthia. He stood up and grabbed her lightly by the arm. Feeling her go stiff, his eyes searched hers. Was she afraid of him? Or was she afraid of being kissed? He hadn't known that her husband had died. What if she was still in love with him? She deserved better than Oliver Brooks, the man that no one could love. She deserved better than the man that killed a child.

Could he be better than that? Could he be someone that she deserved?

Gently, he placed his hand on her cheek. He leaned forward and placed a gentle kiss on her lips, their softness surprising him. As she exhaled gently her lips parted, their light pink buds begging for more.

He leaned in once more and kissed her again. This time he was a little less gentle and a little more demanding. She parted her lips slightly and he entered. His hand on her cheek shifted to slightly behind her head. Her mouth tasted like crisp honeydew and cinnamon. A weird combination, but it compelled him. It called to him in a way unlike anything ever had.

He felt her arms come up and wrap around his waist. His hand gripping her upper arm made it's way to her waist. He slipped it under her shirt, to lightly grab her waist, skin to skin. If only…

The sound of a throat clearing brought him back to himself. They were being watched. Jumping back from her, as if burned, he wondered just how much of a fool he had made of himself. Looking around he noticed that his father had placed a hand over Daniella's eyes and was staring at him in shock. Frank was looking at the floor in embarrassment and Jack was grinning wildly at him.

"Is this a bad time?"

Turning quickly, Oliver came face to face with the jerk of the century, Enrique Montoya, the man that hated people.

"Hey, Montoya." He hated when Oliver called him that, which was one of the reasons he did. "Hey, how's it going?"

"I was told that I needed to see a patient; however, this patient doesn't have any insurance. She needs to go to Saint Luke's and they can handle it from there." There was no hatred lacing his words. In fact, there was no emotion whatsoever. It was like he felt nothing. It was as if nothing could penetrate the steel covering his heart. No water could rust it, never allowing anything through. It was cold and hard. Dead, within his chest.

"Actually, she's my daughter and this is my wife. Per hospital regulations, you have to treat them here at Avalon." The fear threatened to overwhelm him, but putting one over on Montoya made it worthwhile.

A hint of a smile graced Montoya's face before it was masked. It was as if Oliver had imagined it.

"Very well. The MRI that was done this morning didn't reveal anything of significance. However, the patient's white blood cell count is rising. I've done leukemia markers to check to see if it's leukemia. The results should be back soon."

"Dear Lord…"

Oliver turned just in time to catch Synthia as she collapsed to her knees. The sound of them striking the hard floor made Oliver cringe. Montoya wasn't known for his bedside manner, but even he could have done better at breaking this news to a parent. "Synthia. Synthia, come on. It's going to be ok. Everything's fine." He looked at Jack, "Get some ice water."

"No, I'm ok. I just… I just need to sit here for a moment."

She turned as if trying to loosen his hold on her. He gave in and released her, and sat with her on the cold tile floor.

Ignoring Montoya as the man made a quick exit from the room, escorted by Ollie's father and Frank. Montoya would pay for this later.

If it was the last thing he did, Oliver was going to make sure that Montoya knew he needed to treat his patients and their families better than this. Or one day Montoya was going to wake up with his own Lucy Woods and regret it for the rest of his life. Oliver never wanted anyone to go through that… It didn't matter if Montoya was an asshat, he didn't deserve the chilling regret that came with it.

Chapter 9

OLLIE LOOKED AT SYNTHIA LYING behind Daniella, softly stroking her hair. She barely left her daughter's side, and when she did it was because Ollie forced her to take a break.

He began wondering just what she had been through in life. It was hard for him to imagine that she wanted this life, but as he watched her with Daniella… a part of him wished he could crawl on the bed with her and comfort her. He wished he had the right to do it. He wished he had the courage to do it.

"Oliver?"

"Yes?"

"Why are you staring at me?"

Staring? How had she seen him staring? Her gaze was focused on Daniella. "I'm sorry. I just… What do you want out of life?" As the words left his mouth, he wished he could take them back. She flinched and shifted slightly. "I'm sorry, please don't answer that."

"No, it's ok. I don't ever think about what I want." Moving slightly, she sighed. "I used to want a lot of things, but I'm a parent. As a parent, you do what you have to for your kids. Doesn't matter if it's what we want or not. I'm a waitress. Some days I make good money, other days not so much. The team I work with is great. If I need to change a shift then I can. They're all parents themselves and know what it means to have a kid that comes first."

"Where do you work?"

"At a little cafe called Will's Diner."

Oliver scrunched up his face, trying to think of the place. It sounded familiar, like a late night run in between surgeries. "Is it on 32nd street?" At the shocked look she gave him, Oliver assumed that he was right. "That's a nice place, but I don't think I've ever seen you there."

"When have you been there?" Her low tone surprised him. It bordered accusing.

"I don't know…" He didn't really. It was probably after a call in and he was normally on call on Tuesdays. "Maybe a Tuesday night, really late."

"Oh, I don't work then." Relief crossed her face before being replaced by an odd soured look. Something about that night bothered her. Something about that night made her cringe.

"Why is that?"

"When you've been in have you ever seen a guy that's about six feet tall and tan — like, REALLY tan, almost orange?"

He thought about it for a minute and vaguely remembered a jerk that might fit that description. The guy had been practicing sort of grab-assy behavior, something Oliver didn't approve of. He nodded at her.

"He's why I don't work Tuesday evenings. I always have the day shift that day. He followed me home one night." Fear bled through her words, intertwined with each one.

He scrunched up his face and balled his hand into a fist. He didn't trust himself to speak, but knew he had to. "Did he ever hurt you?"

"No, nothing like that…" The way that she paused told Oliver that she was afraid of the tan man, afraid of what he might do if she worked Tuesday evenings. It had gone further than she was willing to admit to him, he could tell. "He is just a creep. I've dealt with them before."

But not like the tan jerk, Ollie could tell. There was something about that particular guy that made her radar ding like a full scale attack. "Has he bothered anyone else?"

"Sheila doesn't work late at night on Tuesdays now either, but she won't talk about it." She sighed deeply and stroked Daniella's hair once more before continuing. "The problem is that we need the money. I'm going to have to take the Tuesday night shift."

"Over my dead body." His tone was harsh, angry almost. He wasn't going to let her take that shift, no matter what.

"Oliver, I'm grateful that you married me so Daniella can be treated, but I need to be able to pay you back. I can't do that if I don't work."

Ollie could tell by the way she set her jaw, stilled her movements, and narrowed her eyes that the matter was not up for discussion. "Very well. I have something that I have to do tomorrow evening too. I'm on call Tuesdays for this month. We rotate, which means I'm on call tomorrow night."

Tuesdays were always harsh. Emergency surgeries only. Anything could happen, and often anything did.

"Jack might be able to watch Daniella for us," he offered, making sure to use the term "us".

He hadn't planned on being married, but if he was going to be married, then he'd be damned if someone laid their hands on his wife.

He'd be damned if his wife didn't understand that he believed in being a cohesive family unit. Daniella might not be his, and they might not have married for love, but he was going to protect her as if she was for as long as he could.

Chapter 10

SYNTHIA FROWNED AS SHE SAW Jacob Jerkowsky walk through Willy's doors. The man was so tanned from that fake tanning stuff that he was orange like a carrot. His black hair was greasy too. His personality was just sleazy.

Synthia hated working Tuesday evenings, but there was no way that she was going to be a freeloader. That's what she felt like with Ollie — a freeloader. The hospital was being wonderful to her and Daniella. People were constantly dropping off food, coloring books, seeing if they needed anything, and saying hi.

It seemed like they were the talk of the place. Synthia still couldn't believe they were married, but she was going to pay Ollie back every dime. It might take her a hundred years, but she was going to do it... even if she had to deal with Jacob the Jerk to be able to.

Stepping up to the table with a pot of coffee in her right hand, she hoped he would behave this time. If not, she'd dump the whole pot in his lap. By accident, of course. "What can I get for you today?"

"Ooh, honey, how 'bout you and Sheila at my place. We could do the tango."

Slime Ball. "Sorry, but I'm not on the menu."

"You'd be amazed at what some money can buy. I'm pretty sure you're within my price range." His words echoed gritty slime, making her feel dirty.

"I am in no man's price range." She ground the words out between clenched teeth.

"I could buy an hour with you for less than you'd think."

Willy, the owner of the diner, hated it when an employee was rude to patrons, but Synthia was done being insulted by that sorry excuse for a man that assumed he could take whatever he wanted. She straightened herself, determined to stand up for herself. "If you're not going to order food, then please leave. You're disturbing the other patrons."

"I'm not disturbing anyone, sexy."

"I have a name," she ground out between clenched teeth. "It's on the badge that you've been staring at since I walked up to the table."

"I'm not staring at your badge…"

"And I'm done here." She turned away from him, to flee from the cockroach.

Smack!

She ground to a halt. Narrowing her eyes, she tightened her grip on the coffee pot. The bastard had smacked her rear…

"Get your ass up!"

Synthia didn't have to turn to know the voice belonged to Oliver, but she did anyway. There was the matter of hot coffee after all. She was going to dump the entire pot over the jerk's nether regions. "Oliver?"

"Synthia get back." Anger rolled off him in waves, threatening to overpower her. His muscles were taunt as violence emanated from him.

"Oliver, please don't!"

"Who the hell is this?" Jacob the Jerk leaned back in the booth. The scum motioned towards Oliver, with a sleazy look on his face. "You gotta boyfriend, tramp?"

"I'm her husband." Oliver's voice boomed throughout the room.

Synthia took a step back. Oliver's face was red, his lips were a tight thin line, and his stance was confrontational. He reminded her of an angry bear, but there was something more… something that made her stomach clench.

"I said get up."

"I'm not in the mood to deal with you. I was negotiating with her."

"We were not negotiating you filthy…"

"Synthia, go in the back."

"I will not."

"Please go in the back. I will come get you in just a minute. You can go all angry on me then, but this jackass will not touch another woman as long as he lives. He will not stare at, leer at, or speak to a woman."

He's going to kill the jerk… The thought frightened her. A tiny part of her was giddy, thrilled at the possibility that the jerk was going to finally get what was coming to him. Not by Ollie though, not by him. And not over her. "Oliver, please… it's not worth it."

"Synthia, you're my wife. I won't have anyone disrespecting you like this."

That's why he was doing this? Because she was his wife? "What do you think you're doing? You're being a troglodyte!"

He smiled, as if he was shocked and pleased that she knew the word.

A sigh came from Jacob. "I just want to use her as a cum bucket for a bit. It's not like I'm going to keep her, you'll get her back."

Oliver lunged at him, swinging, shocking her. Glass shattered, pain seared her leg. As she jumped, her brain vaguely supplied that the coffee pot was no longer in her hand. Instead it was in pieces at her feet, coffee soaking into her legs and shoes.

The sound of flesh hitting flesh made her jump again, propelling her into action. "Oliver! Ollie! Stop!"

A boom of the swinging door slamming into the wall, caused her to spin around. Willy!

"What in the Sam Hill is going on out here?" His voice carried weight, silencing the scuffle.

Synthia swung around. "Willy! Make them stop!"

Willy was a short, slightly balding man in his late fifties. He always wore a baseball cap in the diner. Tattoos of dragons and elves peaked out from beneath his short sleeve t-shirt. He took a step forward and Synthia could see the kitchen door swinging behind him.

He took off the short order cook's apron that he wore around his waist and tossed it on the counter. He swung his baseball cap around backwards. "Who's ass am I about to kick?"

"Willy! It's the jerk!"

Oliver let go of the Jerk's shirt and stepped back. The man grabbed at his bleeding nose.

"Synthia, get in the kitchen," Willy ground out between clenched teeth. His eyes were slightly bloodshot and veins were popping around his temples. She could count on one hand the number of times she had seen him angry… on one finger actually.

This was worse. "Willy…"

"I won't tell you again."

Tears were streaming down her face as she fled into the kitchen, light hiccups escaped from between closed lips. Shame and embarrassment flooded her. The cool metal door swung behind her as she took refuge in the quiet kitchen.

Sizzling bacon, the pop of ham, and the smell of burning pancakes surrounded her. Stepping into the role of cook while Willy handled events in the diner came natural. She reached for the spatula and took a deep breath. Using the hem of her apron, she wiped her tears.

It wouldn't do to cry. Crying was for really bad days. This wasn't a really bad day. Sure, it sucked. It wasn't nearly as bad as it could have been. Daniella was in a good hospital, being treated with lifesaving treatments. That was all that mattered.

Oliver frowned at the door that Synthia had disappeared behind. The tears made him feel like a heel. His mother would have been so upset with him.

"Son, as much as I'm glad to see someone put a wallop on that sorry excuse for a dickwad, I can't let it continue in my diner. It's bad for business." Willy tilted his head towards Jacob.

Oliver looked back at the man in question. Blood poured from his nose, his eyes were wide, and his expression was fearful. The man didn't move or make a sound. "Not that he didn't deserve it, but I think you drilled the point home."

Oliver stepped back from the table. Had he really punched the man? Had he really committed an act of violence because someone was sexually assaulting his wife?

His fists clenched.

Yes, he had.

Was he proud of it? Searching the man's terrified expression, Oliver realized that the man had crossed a line — a line that Oliver couldn't tolerate. He remembered Jack's troubles and was glad that he had stepped in before it went any further. At least he hadn't failed again in that respect.

"Why don't you come over here and we'll talk about it." It wasn't a question. Oliver sighed deeply as he walked towards the counter. "Jacob, I think it's time you find a new place to eat." Jacob got up and ran out of the diner, never looking back.

Willy pointed to a seat at the counter and Oliver obliged. As he sat on the cool bar stool, Oliver wondered just how he had gotten to this point. How had his life gone so awry?

"Folks, I'm sorry that there seems to have been a bit of a show with your dinner. I'm going to give you all a discount on your meal, so order your fill." Once he was done speaking, noses drifted back into menus and voices carried on with conversations that had previously halted. The silence was broken by a cacophony of voices, silverware, and plates.

Willy walked back behind the counter and stood on the other side from Oliver. "Son, you mind telling me what in the sam hill is going on?"

"He sexually assaulted my wife."

"Who's your wife?"

"Synthia."

Willy whistled low and deep, with a mix of awe and knowing. "I'm amazed that you didn't do worse. How's your hand?"

Looking down, he noticed that the flesh was swollen and red around the knuckles. Opening and closing it, he realized that if he was called into surgery it was going to suck. He could still do it, but he'd have to ignore the angry flesh.

"I just need some ice for it, do you have any?"

"For you, I might even throw in a beer."

"I can't. I'm on call at the hospital tonight." He wouldn't dare have anything to drink when he was on call. He rarely drank anything other than water, even soda was off his list of things to drink. It was too sweet and tangy, he just couldn't get used to the taste.

A ringing interrupted him. Grabbing his cell, he felt his gut tighten. The hospital's emergency number glared back at him. It was bad if they were calling him…

"Dr. Brooks."

"Dr. Brooks, we have a problem. There's a code coming in. How long will it take you to get here?" The voice on the other line belonged to Randy, the Administrative Officer of the Day.

"Six minutes, fill me in on the way."

He lowered the phone and looked at Willy. "Please tell Synthia that I had to leave. I'll see her as soon as I can at Daniella's room." Willy nodded and he walked out, raising the phone back to his ear.

"Randy, tell me what we've got."

"Twelve year old. Hit by a car, not wearing a helmet."

A sixty pound weight slammed into his chest, knocking the air from his lungs.

There wouldn't be much he could do, but he would try. Timing was super important. It could decide whether the kid spoke again or whether he walked again. It could even decide if his parents got to say goodbye to him.

Gathering his wits, he put on his doctor face. "Medical status?" As Oliver climbed into his car, he tried to step into the surgeon's shoes. Drawing back from anything not medically relevant was important, was vital.

This was his way of differentiating himself, of standing back enough to have clarity to help his patient. It wouldn't help the kid for him to get emotional.

He had to be clearheaded and focused, he should never

have hit the jerk. His hand was stiff, but it would still work. Just bruising, no damage — no reason to be concerned.

He was the best. This kid deserved the best. They all did.

Chapter 11

"OOF..." THE VOICE STARTLED HER. Looking up Synthia realized it was just Ollie.

As Oliver once again stumbled, Synthia looked him up and down. He was in his scrubs, his face was worn thin. Exhaustion bled from him like a air bleeds from a tire that has a nail in it. "Ollie?"

"Sorry. Is Daniella sleeping?"

"Yes, she was asking for you." She had wanted a story from him, a story about dragons.

"What did you tell her?"

"Why would you think I told her anything otter than the truth?"

"I just figured you were angry with me."

"Enough to lie to my kid?" The very idea was absurd and she could feel her lips curving upward into a smile. She was upset, nuclear was a better word, but her daughter loved him. She wouldn't lie to Dani about him, or anyone.

He shrugged as if it made sense. "Some people do it."

"Well, I told her that you were on call and would be here when you were done taking care of the patient."

"What did she say?"

"That you needed to wake her up, so she could show you her picture."

He aimed a weary smile Daniella's way. Synthia felt her heart beat faster. This man had just dealt with something horrific, the nurse had warned her. He should be screaming to the roof tops in anger, but he was smiling at her daughter. She blinked rapidly to clear the tears threatening to fall.

"Then let's wake her." He walked to the bed, tripping as he went. His shoulders were slumped. The surgery had begun around six pm, it was now four am. "Daniella," he whispered as he knelt beside the bed, placing his elbows on it. He stared at her as she stirred.

"Ollie?"

"Yes, sweetie. Your mama said you wanted to show me something."

"My picture. See it there?" She pointed to the table near the window, it was beside a reclining chair.

"Well, let me take a look."

Synthia watched closely as Oliver went to pick up the picture that Daniella had drawn for him. It was stick figures, three of them. It was them. Would he understand what Daniella thought? What she hoped for?

"Daniella, it's absolutely gorgeous. I love these people. Who is this?" He pointed to the tall one with the weird lines on the face, just squiggly marks in green.

"That's you! You wear a mask when you help people."

"Oh, so this is my mask." He pointed to the lines as if it was plainly clear that it was a mask and not a plague type disease on the stick man's face.

She nodded and yawned.

"It's lovely. Do you think it'd be alright if I put it up in my office?"

"Sure. Mommy puts mine on the fridge. I don't know what an ocif is, but ok."

"It's office, and it's where he works when he's not seeing

THE SURGEON'S DILEMMA 65

patients."

"Oh, are you there a lot?"

"It's where I take my breaks. Your picture would be lovely in a frame up on the wall."

"Ok, then that's good. You can put it there."

He smiled at Daniella and put the picture back on the table. Synthia pushed a lock of hair away from Daniella's face. "Alright, sweetheart, back to sleep for you."

"I love you, mommy."

"I love you too."

"I love you, Ollie."

Oliver was silent and Synthia looked over to see why. She grinned. "Baby, Ollie fell asleep."

"The sandman got to him without us seeing?"

"Sure looks that way." She kissed Dani's head and watched her daughter close her eyes. Looking back to Oliver she stifled a laugh. His head was at a weird angle, he'd have a terrible crick in his neck in the morning, and his mouth was slack. A slight snore came from him. "Good night, Ollie," she whispered.

Turning on her side, she tried to close her eyes, but couldn't. Worry ate at her. Oliver was a good man, but what would happen to them? What was going to happen to Dani? She wasn't going to delude herself into thinking everything was going to be ok. She just had to act like it would be, for Dani.

She sighed softly, wondering about her husband. He had loved them both, even if he and Synthia fought. Could her new husband love her too? Or were they just going to part ways? Could they part ways as friends, or were they doomed? Would Oliver even want to be her friend?

A terrible thought struck her. What if her ruse, and their marriage, had interrupted plans he had with someone else... what if he was already engaged to someone and she caused them grief?

Taking a deep breath, she tried to let the fear slip away from her. She focused on the fact that Oliver hadn't lied to her yet. He would have told her if there was someone else, even if it meant hurting Dani in the process. Stopping, she looked back at him. His jaw was strong, his face was lean, but he was a man. He was a true man. He put his family's needs before his own, whether he realized it or not. He wouldn't have told her. He wouldn't have let her down.

Shame flooded her. It could have ruined his life when she forced herself on him — forced him to marry her.

He shifted, an eye cracking open. "Go to sleep, Synthia. Your thinking is enough to wake the dead."

"Is the kid ok?"

He sighed deeply and leaned back in the chair, kicking it's bottom part out with a spring sound. "We won't know for sure for a few hours… I keep telling parents to make sure their kids are wearing helmets, but they forget just one time. Unfortunately, one time is all it takes. This kid won't be the same. There's so much that can go wrong in injuries like this. There's not enough that can go right. I hope that he'll be ok, but won't know for a while. The nurse may come in and grab me if his condition changes, so try to sleep for a bit."

She heard his frustrations, silent blame for the parents. Did he blame her for Dani?

No, Dani couldn't be fixed if she had worn a helmet. Dani isn't a case of parental oversight. It was easier if you had someone to blame sometimes, whether it was the parent or the doctor. She imagined some of Ollie's patients' blamed him if he couldn't help them. It made her heart feel heavy, knowing that he did nothing wrong, but still had to deal with it…

"Ollie, did I ruin your life?"

"Why would you think that?"

"You never said whether you had someone else or not."

"I'm a surgeon, running a non-profit. When would I have time to date?"

"Are you gay?"

He laughed a soft laugh. "You kissed me, what do you think?"

"I think you tasted pretty good."

"Really?"

"Yes."

"Would you be up to trying it again?"

She thought for a moment. Would it be safe? There was too much going on for her to fall for him, and it would be easy to fall for him. He was sex in a good dream, wound tight and ready to go. He could break every definition that she had on what good sex might be... "We should talk about this tomorrow."

"Too late. We're talking now."

She frowned, realizing that it was a dangerous road, but it was definitely an interesting path to take. "It might be worth pursuing sometime."

"How about tomorrow?" Eagerness and boldness coated his words.

A ripple of desire went through her. It was tiny, like a small rock tossed into a still pond, but it was there. "How about today?" She went still. It was too late to take the words back. They were out there like a bulldozer, ripping through trees to lie down a road — a road that went straight to same the place that heat was pooling, between her thighs.

Shaking herself, she quickly got up from the bed. She couldn't believe herself, flirting with him. What was wrong with her? Her husband hadn't even been in the ground for two years. If that wasn't terrible enough, she was lying in a hospital bed with her little girl, flirting with the man — her husband. She had to remember that's what he was now. He was her husband… and she was his wife.

"Synthia, calm down and lay back down. I'm too tired to ravage you right now, and there's a little girl in the room. We can schedule a time if that'll make you feel better."

Humorous? He found this humorous?

"I'm going to get food. You can watch my daughter for a bit." Without another word she fled the room, leaving the man that made her tingle behind.

The problem was, she really wanted to take him up on his offer. She wanted to feel his hands and his mouth on her skin. She was itching for it, burning up for it. And she had no idea why. Two years and no one had made her feel like this. Two years.

Maybe it had just been too long. Maybe it was just the stress. Maybe it was just him.

Chapter 12

"HEY, OLLIE."

Oliver looked up as Jack entered his office. The man looked so fresh and awake that in that moment Oliver despised him for it. "Hey, they're still sleeping, so I'm getting caught up on some things. I already checked on the kid from last night, he might walk again with some physical therapy. He's actually really lucky that there's no permanent brain damage, just some swelling that's already going down."

He turned and set his coffee back on the desk. "I need to run over to the clinic later. I put a note on the door for now." Looking back at Jack, he realized that something was wrong. No quips, no jokes, no other words had been spoken by his friend...

"Jack?" It was terrifying. Jack wasn't one to be silent unless he had bad news.

Had something happened to Daniella? Was Synthia dealing with it all by herself? What kind of man was he to be sitting there, hiding, while she dealt with it on her own.

Jumping up, he searched Jack's face for any sign of what was going on. Searched it for any hint of what he needed to do — of what he could do.

"Ollie, I'm sorry…"

Oh, God… He raced around his desk toward the door. He had to get to Synthia!

"They know."

The words ground him to a halt. Was he wrong? Were Synthia and Daniella ok?

Ollie's fear started to ebb away. Knew what? The fear slowly began to build again. Had Synthia found out about Lucy?

"Ollie, the board knows about the clinic. I don't know how they found out. I tried to ask, but they shut me down." Jack twisted the hem of his lab coat, wringing it in his hand until it wrinkled.

His shoulder relaxed and slumped. "It's going to be ok. I knew this day might come, but I hoped it never would. I can try to sell the clinic before they do anything about it. Maybe the new owner will still let me work there and keep it on the…"

"Oliver!" Jack interrupted, "You don't understand! You've been called up for a board action. I shouldn't be telling you this, but they're going to vote soon. You're up against a room full of hardasses… They're going to be voting on doing a peer review on all of your cases for the last six months to determine if you did anything wrong because you were moonlighting."

"Is it really moonlighting if I own the place?" How was he going to get out of this? They were going to crucify him…

Jack refused to meet his gaze. "It's a place of competition. According to them, that constitutes as moonlighting."

"But a peer review?" Peer reviews were very serious business. They could cost him his ability to practice medicine. Were they really that upset about it?

"There's more…"

"What?" *More? Really? What else would they do to him?*

Jack shifted from foot to foot, focused on the wall above Ollie, seeing everything but seeing nothing. "If the vote for peer review succeeds, they're going to get Daniella transferred to Saint Luke's if you're found at fault for anything."

This was serious. "Peer reviews take weeks. They'll know more about Daniella's condition by then."

"Ollie, they already established the committee. It's meeting Friday afternoon. They'll remove you if there's any potential fault found." The words were heavy, his tone weary. Jack knew it was serious. He knew Oliver was in the deep end without any way of touching the bottom.

Friday? "Jack, I just need more time."

"You might not be able to save her…" Warning, seared his words.

He was trying to prepare Ollie that not everything broken could be fixed. Not everything damaged could be saved. Not every sick child could be healed.

That option was impossible, it wasn't even allowed in his realm of possibilities. "Yes, I will. I'm not going to let her die like Lucy did!" Lucy dying was his fault, but Daniella wouldn't suffer the same fate. She wouldn't die because someone who could have helped didn't look into everything first.

"Ollie, you might not have a choice in the matter. None of us might have a choice in the matter. I'm sorry, Ollie… it's time for you to learn that sometimes we don't get a choice."

"There's always a choice, always something else we can do."

"No, not always."

Like hell there wasn't. Anger blossomed within him, turning quickly to rage. He wanted the world to burn to ashes, taking all the pain with it. He wanted acid to rain down, scorching his memory of anything bad. He wanted to start over. He wanted a second chance. Problem was, when you take the pain you also take the beauty. Could he survive a second chance if one ever appeared?

He turned and stormed out, slamming the door behind him. He was going to get Daniella the care she needed. He wasn't going to give up. As he stomped down the halls, people stepped out of his way. His face felt hot, like he was feverish or his blood pressure was through the roof. There was only so much that could be done, only so much left to try.

As he turned around the corner to Daniella's room, he saw Montoya standing outside. "Montoya," he ground out. "What is it?"

"Dr. Brooks, I worked very hard for my title. I would appreciate it if you would use it."

"Fat chance in Hell." He itched to take a picture of Montoya's exasperated look. Ollie knew he was baiting him, but he just couldn't help it. He was boiling inside, waiting to rip into someone. It had been a tough surgery with no release of the emotion. It had been an even tougher morning.

Peer review… on all of his cases? All?

Montoya sighed in response. "I was waiting to talk to your wife; however, it seems she is busy at the moment."

"Then talk to me."

"The patient is unfortunately very ill. She will die…"

"Dear God! Is this how you talk to all of your patient's families?" Ollie couldn't imagine what in the world would make the man such a prick. He had been a doctor for a while now, he should know how to speak to patients.

"I do not know any other way to be. Would you rather I give you false hope for her or would you rather I be truthful?"

Ollie stopped, what did he rather? To have the hope that everything would be fine even if it was doomed or to know just how bad it really was? *You can't fix it if you don't know it's broke.* "Fine, tell me how bad it is, but know that I will knock you into next week if you piss me off."

"Touchy are we?"

"Very, so tread lightly."

Montoya nodded. "The patient…"

"Daniella. Her name is Daniella." If the man didn't remember anything else, he was going to remember that. Daniella.

"Daniella has a very rare form of blastoma that has invaded her bone marrow. We're going to begin radiation therapy immediately, despite her illness, but she will need a bone marrow transplant. If she doesn't have one then she won't make it. Her mother isn't a match, I've already had her typed. I did not tell her that was what the purpose of the test was."

Ollie felt like he had been punched in the gut. His legs turned to jelly and he had to grab the wall for support. His stomach threatened to revolt.

She was going to die, just like Lucy had. Only this time, it would be because there were no matches. When the mother wasn't a match, the chances of finding one were reduced significantly. With her father, an orphan, deceased… the chances dropped even further.

"What do I need to do?"

"Let me do what I can. You may think I'm a horrible person, but we both know that I'm the best in my field." His words were sad, with an underlying confidence.

Ollie couldn't argue with him there. It was true. Montoya was the best pediatric oncologist in the US, maybe even the best in the world. If he said to let him work, then

Ollie had to do it.

No matter how much it hurt.

Chapter 13

"HEY, OLLIE. DANIELLA AND I were just talking about you." Synthia knew from the look on his face that something was wrong. Something was frightening and he knew she wasn't going to like it.

She had seen Montoya outside of the room, knew that he was bringing bad news and that he was using Ollie as the messenger. The man had stood staring at her for several minutes before walking away. Twice he had come back. Not once had he come close enough to speak. She stared at him each time, fearful that he would gain his courage to tell her...

She couldn't bear to hear the words from him. She couldn't bear it if he said she was going to lose Dani. She needed just a little bit more normalcy first. Just a few more moments, any that she could get.

But what's normalcy when you're daughter is sick and there's nothing you can do to make it better?

Ollie walked over to Dani, smiling sadly, and gave her a kiss on the head before sitting on the bed beside her. "Hey, sleepyhead. How are you feeling? Is your mommy keeping you company?"

Ollie was perfect with Daniella. She couldn't ask for anyone more perfect. He had a way with her, unlike anyone that she had seen. Her husband hadn't even been able to get her to stop crying. Only Synthia had been able to calm Dani as a baby.

"Yeah, but I want to see Charlie. I think he needs dinner. It's dinner time for fishes."

Her heart clenched. Dani was in a hospital, hooked up to an I.V., And was worried about the stupid goldfish.

"Oh, don't you worry about Charlie. He's going to get fed plenty, I promise. He's going to weigh an extra ten pounds by the time you see him again."

Synthia frowned, he hadn't been to the clinic… He had been with them the whole time. Who was feeding the goldfish? She had a sinking feeling that Charlie wasn't getting fed at all… That Charlie might not be the same on their next visit to the clinic.

"What's on your menu for dinner?" Ollie picked up the piece of paper that had the crayon circles around different pictures of food. Dani had picked her own food.

"Nasty stuff."

The laugh escaped from Synthia before she could stop it. Daniella was right, it looked horrid, but she didn't even know her little girl knew the words to describe something so putrid. The absurdity was amusing to her.

"Sweetheart, would you like something different for dinner?" She couldn't keep the smile from her face.

"No, mommy. I'm not hungry."

"Daniella, you need to eat so you can get strong again." Ollie flexed his muscles at the word strong. Synthia felt her mouth go dry and her insides go warm. "How about if your mommy and I go get you some jello from downstairs? Does that sound good?"

At the hesitant nod, Synthia frowned. If they left, who would sit with Daniella?

"I already called Frank. He said he'd arrange it. The sitter should be here any minute."

As the words were out of his mouth, as if Ollie had summoned him, the door opened and Ollie's dad entered the room.

She watched as Oliver went tense and began opening his mouth to speak. She couldn't take the car wreck about to unfold and decided to intervene before things could get any worse, before Ollie could speak. "Daniella was just talking about how she wanted some jello. Are you sure you're up to watching her for us?"

"Of course I am."

"Thank you, we really appreciate it. I know it was probably a bit unexpected, but it's going to be good for us to get out for a minute. Someone should really do something about improving the food around her." She was rambling, and there wasn't anything she could do to stop it.

"Dear, don't worry about a thing. I was close by actually. I've recently had some meetings in the area. I'm a businessman and I go where the business takes me."

"Alright, as long as it wasn't any trouble." She watched in horror as Ollie began to open his mouth again. "We'll just be in the cafeteria. They can reach us if they need us."

"You'll be fine for a bit. I may be an old man, but I can definitely entertain her by telling her some stories." The smile on his face told her that he was really looking forward to it. He couldn't wait to spend time with Daniella.

"You always were good at the stories," Oliver whispered harshly.

"As I recall, you used to love the one about the Sahara Desert lions, Ollie." His father seemed taken aback by the harsh tone, but determined to ignore it.

"I've grown up since then."

Synthia moved quickly around the bed, kissing Daniella's head and grabbing the tray of nasty food from the rolling tray by the bed. "I think Daniella would love a story. We'll be back soon. Just nothing scary!"

She quickly drug Ollie from the room before things could escalate.

Chapter 14

A S SHE STIRRED HER COFFEE, she surveyed Ollie. His expression was a mix of anger and sadness. "Ollie, what's the deal between you and your father?"

"I don't know what you're talking about." He clammed up and turned his head away from her. His eyebrows furrowed and his lips set in a straight, thin, bloodless line. The anger was winning.

Synthia sighed deeply. He was stubborn, but she had dealt with worse. In fact, her late husband had been well known for his inability to accept a decision, even when he was dying… "Yes, you do. You act like you hate him."

She watched as he sat back in the chair, shoulders slumping as if defeated. "Honestly, I don't hate him. I just don't want to trust him again."

She raised an eyebrow at him in an attempt to convey that she wished for him to continue. When he didn't she waved her hand to prompt him. "And?"

He sighed and scrubbed at his five o'clock shadow, a mix of dark brown and light blond whiskers. He looked exhausted, but it was a special kind of exhaustion. She knew it well. It was mainly from whatever memories he was trapped within. Pain assaulted him. She had seen the look on her own face often enough to recognize it.

"I trusted him and it bit me. I haven't really trusted anyone since, except for close friends. It takes a lot to make me trust."

A thought entered her mind, quick and full of insight. Trust seemed to be his crutch. Trusting himself was his fear.

"Why would you not trust your own father?" Synthia's father lived on the other side of the country, but they still spoke often. She couldn't imagine not trusting him.

"Synthia… my mom… she died when I was just a boy."

"Dear God… I'm so sorry!" Pain assaulted her, on his behalf. She couldn't even begin to imagine what he had gone through as a child losing his mother. As an adult, for her it had been horrible, as a child…

"It's not your fault." He shrugged. "You couldn't have known. My father betrayed me. He tossed me in boarding school after my mother died and left me there to rot."

The words were strangely void of emotion, as if he had rehearsed them many times before in an attempt to remove all emotion from the words. It was as if they were so practiced that they came from someone else, someone that didn't live that life.

"Did you consider that he didn't know what to do with you? He might not have known just what all came with being a father," she suggested.

"He knew." The anger was back. "My grandfather was a great man. My father just became a little lacking."

"He lost his wife. When I lost my husband… the world stopped. It took everything I had just to get up from the bed, just to quit crying long enough to take care of Dani. Grief is a powerful thing. I think you're underestimating it." Her grief had almost broken her. Words couldn't describe how much she had wanted to give up. If they hadn't had Dani, then she wouldn't have been able to continue on.

"My mother died. How am I underestimating it?" His words were sneered slightly.

She could tell that he found no comfort in her words. Maybe it was too much to try to explain, or maybe she was explaining it wrong.

"You're forgetting that you were young, you were…" She struggled for the right word. It was hard to choose one that wouldn't be hurtful. "You were flexible. Your father? That was his life and his life was gone. I know firsthand what that feels like…"

"I think we should talk about something else." His words left no room for discussion, they were full of finality and promise.

She would drop it for now, but she was determined to bring it up again in the future. "Fine. Why don't you tell me what Montoya said to you that freaked you out so bad."

☾

How could he tell her that Montoya believed that it was… just a matter of time before Daniella died, unless she got the transplant? This was her baby, her child. This was all that she had left of her husband…

"Are you going to tell me or are you just going to keep looking at me with that forlorn look on your face?"

"I'm trying to think of the best way to tell you without worrying you."

Her body seized up and she sat up straight. She had gone from friendly to frigid in two seconds flat. The arctic wind had arrived and destroyed the flowers of spring.

There was no easy way to say it… "Synthia, Daniella needs a transplant."

"Why? What kind of transplant? Can I give it to her? How dangerous is it? When will they do it?"

The questions flew from her and Ollie was impressed. She hadn't bemoaned or wailed at the horrible circumstances. Instead she wanted information. With information you can make decisions. He could give her all of the information she needed, that he was good at.

"I'm going to tell you everything I can, then you can ask all of the questions you have, ok?"

She nodded feverishly at him.

"She has a rare type of cancer that's destroying her bone marrow. That means her bone marrow is replicating in a bad way and hurting her. She can't fight infections because of it. Right now it looks like it's just in her bone marrow, it hasn't metastasized, or spread."

He watched her to make sure she was still focused, and she was. Her eyes were wide, frightened orbs aimed at him. There wasn't a chance of her missing a single word he said. Her determination astounded him. She was ready and willing to fight, and it seemed she always had been. He was impressed.

"Montoya typed you to see if you're a match. I'm sorry, but you're not."

A tiny sound escaped her, and Ollie watched closely to make sure she was ok. The sound was a strangled cry, but she pulled herself together. People continued to walk about the cafeteria, oblivious to the fact that Ollie was giving Synthia the worst news a parent could get... Well, almost the worst news...

"She's being put on a list. They're going to do everything that they can to find her a donor. If they can find her one then there will be a bunch of tests that have to be done before the transplant can occur. They're going to have to kill off Dani's immune system to keep it from rejecting the donor's marrow."

"Is that painful?"

"I'm not going to lie to you. It can be, but they'll make her as comfortable as they can. They want her to succeed. They want her to get well..." He refused to tell Synthia that they wanted Dani to live. While it was true, it would be hurtful. He needed her to have hope, to believe that everything would be ok. If she believed it, he could too.

"She will get well. How long will it take for them to get her a donor?"

How could he put a time limit on that? It could be days, it could be years. There was even a chance that one would never come. If her typing was as rare as it seemed, then it was possible that it would be too late... "It might take some time, but they'll keep us up to date. They'll make sure we know."

"We?"

"Yes, we're a we now. You're my wife. Dani is my kid. They're going to treat you both like family because you're my family."

"What happens when Dani's well?"

"What do you mean?" Her cautious tone confused him. What could she mean? When Dani got well, they left the hospital.

"Well, this isn't forever, right? You're going to let me go after she's well... aren't you?" Her shy tone told Oliver that she was truly concerned about what would happen, but not with Dani's illness.

She was concerned about what would happen with them. She was concerned that he wouldn't let her go. Did she think he was a monster?

"If you want an annulment we can get one. If you want to stay married until you're finished with all of her check ups then it's going to be a few years. We'll have to get a divorce."

"Don't you dare think I'm going to try to take anything from you in it!"

Her tone shocked him. It was as if she was scandalized at the mere thought of it, but he hadn't even mentioned it. "What are you talking about, Synthia?"

"I'm not a gold digger."

"Who said you were?"

"I just want you to understand that if we continue with this charade then it's not because I want to take you to some crazy place and take all of your money."

Crazy place? What on Earth? Realization dawned on him. "The expression you're searching for is "take you to the cleaners", but I don't know why you would think I'm concerned about that..." Her misuse of the phrase brought a half smile to his face. She was a unique individual, nothing he had ever expected to encounter.

"Well, it just seemed natural that you would be. I mean, isn't that what people do in divorces?"

That's what she thought? "Synthia, you need to understand that I don't care about that. If you need money then take it. We do need to talk about one thing though..."

The look she gave him was shy and hesitant, worried almost. "What?"

"We need to talk about moving you guys' belongings to my place. I'm not going to have you living in the gas lamp district while Dani is going through all of these treatments. It's too dangerous. I want you to be safe."

"Why?"

"You're my wife. It wouldn't look good if you were living somewhere else, now would it?"

If he was being honest with himself, it wouldn't be acceptable for her to live somewhere else. He still remembered the taste of her lips. He still remembered the soft caress of her hand on his, the feel of her hips beneath his hands. If he was being honest with himself, he would admit that he was hoping for another kiss. Being honest with himself would only get him in trouble — if she knew how his mind was working, what it was focusing on.

"I guess. We need to have ground rules." The words were spoken with an easy tone, but there was tension underneath.

His lips curved upwards in a smile. Of course she would want some ground rules. Ground rules were important for her. Life was chaos, rules just made one feel in charge of the mess. It was like a thousand puzzle pieces. Organizing them by pulling the edges out gave a starting point. She was just looking for her starting point.

"What kind of ground rules would you like?"

"Can we go somewhere else to talk about it?"

"Sure, we can go to my office. Just let me get Dani's jello. We'll take it to her and then go to my office."

Chapter 15

STANDING IN OLLIE'S OFFICE, SHE felt out of place. The lights were off, but the sun filtered through the window blinds. It was peaceful, calm. It was how she wanted to be.

As Ollie went around the desk to check his emails she went to close the door. Quietly, she clicked the lock in place. Turning back to him, she studied him. He was kind, sweet, and loving. Whether he wanted to admit it or not.

He was doing everything he could to make sure Dani was taken care of, even keeping the painful truth from her. Her throat clenched. Emotion, raw and sharp like glass, was stuck in it.

She just wanted a few minutes, a few minutes, of freedom from it. She just wanted to be held and told that everything would be alright. She just wanted to be distracted.

Walking around the desk, she took a deep breath. Just because it had been two years, didn't mean that she couldn't still feel her way around a man. It didn't mean that she couldn't still seduce a man. She just hoped this man wanted to be seduced.

"Synthia?"

"It's tomorrow."

"What?"

"It's tomorrow. We decided that we were going to try the kissing thing again tomorrow, which is today."

"I would love to, but I think you're a bit upset right now. I don't want you to regret it."

"Oh, God. You don't want me." Mortified, she stumbled back away from him.

"No! No, that's not it!"

"This was a bad idea."

"No." He grabbed her by her upper arm, stopping her from fleeing any further. "Synthia, I want you, but I don't want it to just be an escape."

"You don't want what…? Don't you know that sex is about escaping things? Sex can be many things. It can be used to make you feel good when you don't. It can be used for confidence. It can be used for love. It can be used for tons of things."

"I thought you just wanted to kiss me."

The smirk on his face made her want to storm out in a dramatic fashion. He was right though. She had changed to sex, from a kiss.

"Fine, I want you to have sex with me." She held up a finger to silence him. "Not because of what's going on, but because I have something in my system for you and I need to get it out."

The grin he gave her made her belly drop. It was sin, and she wanted it. She ached for it. What she wouldn't give to know what he would feel like inside of her…

"Synthia, are you sure?"

"Kiss me and find out for yourself…"

Before she could finish, his hands were on her and his lips were touching hers. Hazelnut, the taste was still on his lips from his coffee creamer.

One hand grabbed lightly at her waist. The other was

clenched in her hair at the base of her neck. The strange sensation of tightness it gave made her wet. It pooled between her thighs, making her ache for more.

His tongue prodded gently at her lips, begging entrance. Parting them, she was unprepared for the sensation of his tongue running along hers. Her knees buckled. Ollie caught her. Breaking the kiss, he grinned at her before picking her up. Swinging her legs around his waist, she locked herself around him, aching for whatever was to come.

Tilting her head back, she moaned as he began dropping light kisses on her skin. He followed them by a tiny sucking kiss. He was marking her neck and her chest. A throb began in her vagina. The ache grew.

She felt the desk at her back as Ollie leaned her over it, gently laying her on it. He leaned back and pulled off his t-shirt, revealing tight abs. An overwhelming desire came over her to reach up and lick them. She did. Her tongue glided across the smooth expanse and he shuddered, a strangled sound escaped from him.

"Was that ok?"

"Ok? Hon, that was better than ok."

She grinned and did it again.

"You're going to have to stop that or this is going to go quicker than we'd both like. I'm dying to be inside of you. I like the idea of foreplay though."

"I'm not much into foreplay. I'd much rather get to the good stuff." She never had been either, always enjoying the sensations of the act much more than anything leading up to it.

He looked shocked at her words. She sat up straight and pulled her shirt over her head. Sitting on his desk, in her bra and sweatpants made her feel powerful. She kicked off her shoes before slipping off her sweatpants. Clad in nothing but her underwear had never made her feel more in control.

Ollie looked her up and down, licking his lips. Her lips curved upward in a smile. She still had the ability to make a man desire her. "Are you going to fuck me or not?" The word sounded unfamiliar on her tongue, but it had the desired effect. He pushed his jeans down, pushed her back on the desk, and began raiding her with his mouth again.

She pulled her legs up and crossed the behind him, holding him to her. She felt him reach down and push her panties to the side. She felt his member at her entrance.

Her body was so tight. So ready. If only he would enter her. "Ollie!"

She felt his grin against her skin, as he began to slowly enter her. Stretching her, inch by inch, until she couldn't take it anymore.

"If you don't hurry it up, I'm going to take charge."

"Take charge then."

Glaring at him, she used her legs that were still locked around him and forced him forward, sending him into her fully. She shuddered in delight at the sensation of being filled. Mumbling incoherently, she waited for him to begin moving again.

Slowly, out and in, he moved.

Desire threatened to overwhelm her and burn her from the inside out. She began rocking against him as his pace increased. Her eyes were closed, it was too intense to keep them open.

A moan tore loose from her as he thrust harder into her. Harder and faster. Filling her in a delicious way with each thrust. The spiral of emotions took her higher. Her body clenched, she dug her nails into his skin. The orgasm that had been building, ripped from her, threatening to consume her in a blazing inferno. Her mouth opened in a silent scream. She was coming. Her muscles clenched, relaxed, clenched, relaxed. A spasm of emotions, cascading touches tore through her.

Opening her eyes, she saw Ollie's head thrust back, and realized he was coming too. A smile graced her lips, pride filled her.

She felt him fill her as her body still shook. Her skin tingled from the high.

He stayed buried within her as he looked down at her, a smile aimed at her.

As she was still in the euphoria of the orgasm, she realized her heart had crossed a dangerous line. Somehow it had crossed into enemy territory and she had fallen for Ollie. She had fallen hard.

Love, she loved him. And it was the scariest thing that had ever happened to her.

$$Chapter\ 16$$

LOOKING AROUND THE ROOM, SYNTHIA felt out of place. People were making decisions and not keeping her in the loop. They went to Ollie for it all.

But she was Dani's mom.

Ollie had married her, sure, and she was grateful for that. However, he was going to leave them sooner or later. If that wasn't painful enough, it didn't help that she enjoyed that kiss and the sex.

That kiss…

It was like a sugary treat on a hot long day, after working the late shift at the diner. It was a moment in time that she wanted to replay over and over again. It was… it was great.

The sex…

It was even better. It was like Chinese New Year, complete with fireworks and Moon Cakes. It was the thrill she felt in college when she was learning something new. It was something that she'd never be able to forget.

The problem was, it couldn't ever happen again. If it did, then she wouldn't be able to tell him no. She wouldn't be able to leave him once Dani got better because… Because she had done something crazy and fallen in love with him.

Willy would give her hell if she and Ollie split, if he

found out she loved Ollie. Her father would be ecstatic. The man would love her getting married again, maybe she'd tell him soon.

She sighed deeply. How was she going to tell her father that she married a man for her child? That she married a man she didn't love?

It was time she called him and told him. These guys didn't need her in the room anyway. She glanced towards Ollie and made a motion that she was going to step outside. He nodded and went back to his conversation with the nurse. He'd fill her in later, not holding anything back because she'd asked him not to.

Slipping quietly out of the room, she felt some of the pressure melt away. Dani was getting worse. They needed to find her a donor soon.

Wandering down the hall, she found the phone on the wall, the one they let her use before. It didn't need a special code to call long distance. She dialed the number etched in her memory. It rang twice, an old fashioned ring.

"Hello?" The voice made her heart jump, her throat clog, and everything seem ok. It was a long lost hug just waiting for her.

"Dad, it's me." Her voice was a whisper as she struggled to keep the emotion from it.

"Hey, baby. How's my grand baby? Is she getting better?"

"Dani's real sick, Pops."

"I know, but she's going to be ok. You said she's in a good hospital. They'll look after her. Don't you worry." He was so confident. She wished she was too.

"Dad, I don't know what to do. I… I did something horrible. I did something terrible and I can't undo it." Her voice broke, tremors flooded her as she stifled the sobs threatening to tear clear from her. Big nasty sobs that would rack her whole body. She'd had them before, when her husband died.

"Baby, if you need me to come there you just say so. I'll find a way."

"No, Dad. It's not that. It's just… I got married to a guy…"

"Married? You got married and didn't call me?" There was humor to his words, no hurt laced them. Her father was a good man, but he knew she wouldn't have done it unless she had to.

"I had to do it quickly…" It was now or never. "He put Dani on his insurance. She's getting treatment at a good hospital because of it…"

"Do you love him?"

The question was simple but the answer was far from it. The answer to the number of days in ten light years was more simple that that question. She at least knew about light years. She had wanted to be so much more than a waitress… once upon a time. Dreams die when you have a family to take care of. Her husband hadn't wanted a physicist wife, he'd wanted a stay at home one. She had loved him, so she did. Dropped out of school for him.

"Sweetheart, I asked if you love him…?"

"I don't know. I think I do, but I don't know."

"Baby, it's a simple question. You either do or you don't."

"I do. God help me, I do. I don't even know how it happened."

The laugh startled her. Her father was laughing at her. "If only your mother was alive to see this!"

"What?"

"She would love this. Our baby girl finally fell in love."

"Dad, I loved my husband."

"That guy was a jerk. You just thought you loved him. Love is sneaky. One minute you're like 'Oh, that's a fine lady that I could have some fun with' and the next it's 'I'm going to marry this woman and have kids with her because she's the best thing ever'. Love is crazy, but it's a wild ride."

"When did you know you loved Mom?"

"I knew the day I met her. She told me I wasn't ever going to amount to anything if I didn't take her to the formal." Synthia grinned. It was just like her mother to say that. "She was right too, that woman was always right."

"Do you miss her, Dad? I miss her."

"Baby, I miss her, but I know I'm going to see her again one day. That's worth it to me. Your guy, is he a good man?"

"He's Dani's pediatrician... Well, he's the doctor that works at the clinic..." Ollie was a neurosurgeon, not a pediatrician. He'd never lied and said he was one though. In fact, he hadn't lied to her once. "Yes, he's a good man." She said it with conviction.

"That's good. What does he want from you?"

Thinking about it, she realized that Ollie hadn't asked for a single thing in return. "Honestly, I don't have a clue. I was worried for a bit that he might want something that I couldn't give, but he just seems to want Dani to get better... Is that crazy?"

"I'd ask him why. It might be that he has a reason for it... Might have a need to see her well."

True, there was something in his past that he wasn't telling her, something driving him down a destructive spiral. Could it be stopped? Or would he take her crashing and burning with him? If it saved Dani could she handle it? Would she want to? Or would it be worse than it was before?

"What's his name?"

"Oliver Brooks."

"That name sounds familiar to me, but I can't place it."

"I may have mentioned it before…"

"No," her father interrupted. He wasn't one to interrupt her. Not even when she was shouting to the rooftops that she was running away to get married whether he liked it or not. Not even when she was asking her father how to get a divorce, before her husband died.

"Are you sure?"

"I'm sure. I'd remember if it you mentioned it. You're a good kid. I know you'll do the right thing. If you think this is necessary to save Dani, then I'll support you. I'm sorry that I missed the chance to see you down the aisle, but I'm just not getting around like I used to.

He wasn't either. She knew how much it cost him just to get to the phone when she called. He loved her and would do anything for her, but she wouldn't ask him to do that at the cost of his health. Maybe one day soon she could get Dani well enough to go visit him.

"When Dani gets well we're going to come see you." She'd find a way to make it happen. Ollie had already done so much for her, she wouldn't ask him for the money. Maybe she could get a second job? Maybe the hospital needed help in the cafeteria? She could cook, she'd done it at the diner a time or two. If they'd hire her, she'd clean floors at night while Dani slept if she had to.

"I'd like that, but I don't want you to go through any trouble to get here. You hear me?"

She loved her father, but wouldn't admit to it being any trouble at all. "I won't, I promise." That was one promise she would gladly break.

"Synthia?" She turned and saw Ollie standing in the hallway, calling her name.

Chapter 17

OLLIE FELT LIKE A TWO ton weight of wet cement had landed on him, gooey and frozen like quicksand and ice all at once. She had been on the phone to someone, someone he shouldn't be eavesdropping on her talking to. Was it a lover?

Synthia stared at him, probably waiting for him to speak. His mind was trapped on the thought that she might have a lover. His wife might have a lover... What should he do? How do normal people handle it when their wives have lovers.

The absurdity of the thought caused him to laugh, drawing a concerned look from Synthia. Who in their right mind would want to know how normal people handled their wives having lovers? A normal person would go for divorce, or attempted homicide.

Their marriage was far from normal. Their lives were far from normal. Normal was an illusion that people used to tell themselves everything was ok. Normal was the dreamland one saw when they slept. Normal wasn't real.

"Ollie?"

He took a deep breath and stepped toward her, trying to reign in his thoughts and fix his face. *Be the doctor*, he chanted in his head. *Be the doctor she needs.*

Stepping up to her, he noticed the phone dangling from her fingers, it's bright blue color contrasted her skin but matched her cheap bracelet. "Do you need to finish your call?"

She pulled the phone back to her ear, "Dad! I'm sorry! They were calling me and I set the phone down… No, no, everything's ok. It's just Ollie… Yes, my husband."

Dad? She was on the phone to her father? And she just told him that she was married…

Shit.

Shit.

Shit.

This was going downhill fast.

What kind of man was her father? Would he rake Oliver over the coals of an ancient grill or one of those fancy new ones with the extra burners on the side? Would he warm it up first or use a gallon of lighter fluid?

"Sure, you can talk to him."

Shit. It just got worse.

He shook his head, looking at the phone like it was a rattler poised to strike.

"Ollie, it's just my dad." As she handed him the phone, he swallowed deeply. It was her father, whom Oliver assumed was important to her. It was a man that she possibly respected and loved. Why hadn't he asked?

"Yes?" His voice was hesitant and weak. All the confidence of the surgeon had fled faster than the first spring flower once the last frost hit it. He cleared his throat and tried again. "Yes, sir?"

"You that fancy doctor guy that married my little girl?" The voice reminded him of one of the teachers at his second boarding school. The teacher had told him that he had a choice. He could make something of himself, or he could end up dead on the street. Ollie chose to make something of himself and became a doctor because of that teacher.

"Yes, sir."

"You looking after my grand baby?"

"Yes, sir."

"You going to take care of them?"

"Yes, sir." It was easier to stick with the one word answers. It was even easier to add the polite term of sir to each one. The man could be ten feet tall, four hundred pounds for all Oliver knew. Or he could be bound to a wheelchair, febrile from illness. You never knew, but with a commanding voice, it was easier to be polite.

"Good, then I guess you'll do."

"Do for what?"

"For a husband for my baby. She needs a new one. The last was lacking, in my opinion. Prick made her leave a promising career as a physicist to be a housewife. Then the son of a bitch died on her. No good in my opinion. You better be better than that. Course the sorry louse gave me a grand baby before he kicked up those silly flower thingies."

"Daisies?"

"Yep, those are the ones."

"I'm not sure I'm much better than him, but I can try to be."

"Son, there's no try in this. Marriage is for life. Last one died. You can too. If you screw up, I won't make it quick."

"Did you kill the last one?"

"Nah, but I will kill you."

Oliver swallowed a heady breath, his breakfast of eggs turned sour in his stomach.

"Son, you gotta understand… I don't have much life left. I can sit in a prison or I can sit at home. It doesn't matter much to me. Prison has crappy food, but they have cable. That counts for something."

Cable? The man tried to decide whether prison was worth it by whether they had cable or not?

He believed the man when he said he'd kill him. What man threw out random threats on someone's life if he wasn't prepared to carry through. Strangely enough, he liked Synthia's dad.

"I'll keep that in mind."

"Now, you go take care of my baby and my grand baby. Also, have her email me a picture of you. I need it for when I have to contact the mob about you." A low laugh sounded through the earpiece of the phone before the line went dead.

Synthia stood in front of him, grinning like a loon. She had heard every word of it. Oliver was sure.

"Is your dad crazy?"

"Not a bit. Most serious man that I know. Shot a bb gun at my prom date long ago. Guy still doesn't walk right."

Chapter 18

FRANK GLARED AT HIM. THE Chaplain was angry with him. Ollie had managed to piss off a man of the cloth.

He was going to Hell.

His father's best friend, the man that had been there for him after his mother died, the man that had bailed him out of jail... that man, was steaming mad. That man was angrier than Ollie had ever seen him. That man had sat aside his Chaplain title and decided enough was enough.

He was going to Hell and it was going to be paved with every memory of his childhood, every memory where Frank had laughed off something hurtful that Ollie had done.

"Frank, all I'm saying is that I don't need to talk to the man."

"That's hogwash. You have no idea how much you need to talk to him. He's doing everything he can to make things up to you and you just keep throwing old things in his face. When are you going to grow up?"

This was coming from the same guy that had taught him how to hock a loogey when he was seven.

"Grow up? You think I need to grow up?"

"Yes! You had a crappy thing happen, now go be a man

and talk to your father." Like it was really that simple. Like it was really something so easy that could be done without any emotion. Like it was really something where one could just push away the past and pretend like it never happened.

"Like Hell." Oliver turned on his heel and stormed out of Frank's office. Flexing his hands to try to calm himself, he felt like he was going to explode. His heart was beating a fast steady drum within his chest, the pace quick enough to power a small country if bio power was a thing.

Frank might mean well, but he needed to understand that Ollie couldn't take any more. His cup was full and running over onto the table. His sandbox was wet and his castles had been knocked down. There was nothing left, no space unturned where emotions could be boxed up and hidden from the world.

All his boxes were cracking and breaking, leaking pent up emotion on to the world.

It was all too much.

They were going to be voting any minute on whether to peer review his cases, Dani was getting worse, and now Frank tried to intervene and make him talk to his father. It all started with Lucy. It all went back to Lucy. It was a vicious cycle that never seemed to end. History was repeating itself and once again there wasn't anything he could do to stop it.

Stopping in the middle of the walkway that crossed over the street he turned toward the glass, looking out over the city streets. He gripped the thick round metal railing, wringing it with all his strength.

He closed his eyes and tried to take deep breaths.

The clinic was going to close. Dani was going to die. Synthia… would never forgive him.

It was just too much. It was too fast. There wasn't anything he could do.

Ollie felt like he was being torn apart, with no hope of ever being made whole again. Nothing would ever be the same. Unless he found a way to fix it before the vote.

Opening his eyes, he looked out at the city. Cars drove under the crosswalk, oblivious to his torment. The sun was rising high in the sky, light glinting off of glass buildings. People milled about below. Their lives were fine. Their lives were normal. Ollie's was broken.

They were probably happy, content even, with what was going on in their lives. Ollie was jealous of them. Jealousy was a nasty thing too. Once it climbed out of the box there was no going back in, no going back to the way things were before.

Why couldn't he be content? Why couldn't he be happy? Why couldn't he just have fun?

Because a little girl, now his daughter, needed his help.

She needed him, like no one ever had ever needed him. Synthia needed him too. If he didn't find a way to help them, then the life he had was going to be worthless. It was all coming to this moment, whether he realized it or not…

He was going to have to go see his father.

It was the only way. He was going to have to go see the man that forgot about him. He was going to have to ask him for help.

The very thought of asking him for anything sickened Ollie. It made his blood boil and his head ache. However, he would do it for Synthia and for Dani. He would do it for them.

Chapter 19

OLLIE SAT IN THE OVERSTUFFED, uncomfortable chair in the library of his father's mansion. A painting of his mother hung over the fireplace. She was smiling, just like he remembered. Her smile was like the golden fleece, making everything better. This room didn't deserve to have her smile in it. This room was his father's.

"Ollie, why won't you talk to me?" His father sat in the chair across from him, a cup of tea in his hands. His dull gray sweater made his face look older than Ollie remembered it.

His father's question was sincere, but it rankled Ollie. Did the man truly not know what he had done? Did he truly have no clue that Ollie regretted him? All he ever wanted was his mother back, and his father to be there for him.

"Dad, I haven't been able to talk to you since mom died! It was like you just couldn't stand to look at me. You shipped me off to boarding schools the first chance you got and never came back! I've made myself into a good man. No one else can claim responsibility for that. No one."

They couldn't either. Ollie had made sure of that. He had done it all on his own. He had sat through classes, taken tests, done his own projects, etc. He had done every-thing to get several degrees, graduate with honors, and land a prestigious residency. That residency had gotten him where he was, Avalon. He had done it all on his own.

"Here you are asking me for help and screaming at me that I haven't been there for you." His father shook his head. "Well, son, you can't have it both ways. Either I'm there for you or I'm not. One day you're going to have to realize that I lost my wife. I lost the woman I loved more than life itself. She died and I couldn't handle it."

"One day you're going to have to realize that I lost my mother. Then I lost my father because he couldn't handle it!" The words came out as a snarling jumbled mess, but he meant them. He had been waiting to say them for years, bottling them up under the top was too tight to stay on anymore.

Jumping up from the chair, he realized that staying there, arguing with his father, wasn't worth it. It wasn't going to change anything. It was just a waste of his time.

Ollie turned on his heel and walked out of his father's mansion, ignoring his name being called. It was just a memory of the past. There was a time when everything had to end, a time to give up and quit fighting. It was time for him to give up on his father… it was time for him to give up on the things he wanted in life.

A chirp like ring tone sounded from his pocket. Pulling out his phone he looked hard at the face. It was Synthia calling him. It was time to be a man. It was time to stand up for what was right.

He was going to force Avalon to handle Daniella's case, despite how upset they were with him over the clinic. He'd give up his career, but he was going to save her first. He had money. At fifteen he had hired a stockbroker. He could pull it all out. He might have to close down the clinic, but Daniella would live. Grit and determination had gotten him through life. It wasn't about to fail him now.

As he answered her call, he felt empowered in a way that he hadn't in so long. "Synthia, I'm on my way."

"There's a man here from a donation place. He's asking all kinds of questions… I don't know the answers."

Donation place? Could it be… did they find a donor?

"Put him on the phone."

"Hello?"

"You're speaking to Dr. Oliver Brooks. What are you asking my wife?"

"Oh, Hey, Dr. Brooks! This is Sam. I had heard you got married, but I didn't know this was your wife. Congratulations! I was asked to come brief her on the bone marrow donation process."

"Why?"

"Dr. Montoya hasn't told you yet?"

"No, he hasn't." And Ollie was going to strangle him for not telling him.

"He found a donor for your daughter. The donor is going through the final process now. It's all in house, so we can have it done very quickly. Could have it done as early as Monday."

That was just a few days away. "Where did the donor come from?"

"Dr. Montoya said that the guy has been registered for a while, but wasn't a match to anyone that needed a donor until now. He got matched by accident too. The computer dinged it up just minutes ago." He heard the phone being shuffled before the guy continued. "Everything's in order, but I need your wife to consent. Dr. Montoya wanted the husband to consent too, but he didn't say that was you."

Of course he didn't. He wouldn't want Oliver's job to

be in the way of the process. "I'm off site right now, but I'm on my way. Can you wait about fifteen minutes?"

"Sure, I can leave some papers with your wife and come back. The donor's not going anywhere. He was really specific about who could have his bone marrow. He wanted it to go to kids. He's refused all adults. Has a soft spot for them or something. Not real sure."

Oliver frowned, but ignored the flags that raised. Some people were just odd or some had even lost loved ones that were children because a match was never found. The donor was probably one of those. At least Oliver hoped he was. That would make him feel much more at ease. "Go ahead and leave the paperwork. She and I will discuss it when I arrive."

"Sure thing, bye, Doc."

As Oliver hung up, he took a deep breath before making his next call. It was answered on the third ring. "Josh."

"You still haven't learned how to properly answer a phone." He smiled. Josh never would learn. He was old school and wasn't about to change for anyone. That was why Oliver liked him.

"Hey, kid! How are you doing?"

"Good. You?"

"Well, I was better before you called. You sound down. It's like you're thinking something bad, kid."

He got behind the wheel of his car and shut the door, starting it before he finally spoke. "Josh, Avalon found out about the clinic. I'm in trouble. I need to know what to do. What do I do?"

"Damn, kid. I knew this would come. Let me make some calls. It'll be ok."

"I got married, Josh. I'm a dad to a kid that's dying. She needs a bone marrow transplant. If she doesn't get it then she's done. If they fire me, then they will try to deny her treatment. They'll send her to Saint Luke's… I'll need to pay for it all out of pocket or she's going to die…" There wouldn't be anything that could save her if she didn't get the bone marrow transplant. "She's just a kid for God's sake!" Tears of frustration streamed down his cheeks.

"Do you even know how much that will cost?"

Oliver did. It was hundreds of thousands of dollars. That wasn't taking into account any of the follow up care she would need…

"Of course you do. Honestly, I don't know if you have enough in your funds that I can liquidate that quick. Kid, give me a few hours. I'll do my best to see what I can do. Can you hold them off until then?"

Could he? He would stage a coup if he had to.

"I'll avoid the board members like the plague. As long as the Chief of Staff or HR doesn't find me then I'm good."

"Give me at least five hours."

"I can give you four."

"Do your best to give me five. It takes time to trade."

"Do your best." If Josh couldn't get him the money then Ollie would rob a bank. It didn't matter now. His career was over, the clinic was gone… After all of these years, he was still screwing up. He would save Dani if it was the last thing he did. He just needed to make sure they didn't find out if he robbed the bank. That was possible, right?

Chapter 20

THE CHIEF OF STAFF STOOD in front of him, blocking his path to Dani's room, cutting off his route. The man, Dr. George O'Hare, was only fifty-two, but was a shark. That's how he got to be where he was, making decisions that had life or death consequences based on what was best for the patient. And he was good at it.

Every clinical person fell under him, even Ollie.

"Oliver, I need to speak with you." George's voice had a rough edge to it.

Oliver should have expected that he would be waiting at Dani's room for him. Of course he would have found out too. If everyone else knew, of course he did too. "Can it wait?"

"I'm afraid not. I'd much rather not do this in front of your family." Hope that he could give Josh the time he needed died a quick and painful death. It was too late. The word family was stressed as if he knew that Oliver had done something wrong. George turned and walked away, clearly expecting Oliver to follow, which he did.

As they entered George's office, Oliver felt as if he

was done. He hadn't been able to give Josh the time he needed. He was going to have to figure other ways of getting Dani's transplant done. Synthia trusted him and he wasn't going to let her down.

He began going over things in his mind. Turning plans and plots over and over, looking for one that might succeed. If he couldn't rob a bank then there had to be a way that he could stall them… There were ten guards on shift at any time. It would take them at least four minutes to respond to a Code Juliet…

"Whatever you're thinking, you need to put it out of your mind. Don't make this worse than it already is." George pointed to one of the terribly stiff, faded green faux leather chairs. They were known as the Chairs of Doom amongst all of the clinical people that fell under George. It was the last stop seat, the last stop before getting your little cardboard box…

Ollie hung his head. "Have a seat, Oliver."

There would be no Code Juliet, just like there'd be no robbing a bank. He wasn't capable of committing a criminal act. Well, he could punch an idiot, but that was about it. "George, I already know what this is about. Can we please just skip that. Formalities will just make it worse."

"I'd rather you sit." It wasn't a request to placate an old man. In fact, it wasn't a request at all. It was a demand — a demand spoken with the confidence of a man that had survived worse than Ollie could ever throw at him.

They walked over to the round meeting table set in the middle of the Chairs of Doom in the corner of George's office. It was a round table, mimicked on the tale of King Arthur's Court. However, Oliver didn't feel very equal in that moment. As they sat, Oliver realized George was getting comfortable, stretching out the seconds into minutes before he spoke, as if he was considering his words with the utmost care.

"George, I'm an adult. I can take it." It was painful just uttering the words, but it was true. He could take it. Frank was right, it was time he grew up. It was time he became the man that Dani and Synthia needed.

Dani was a sweet kid. He hoped she remembered him after Synthia left him. Maybe she'd even let him say hi on special occasions...

"Oliver, I've watched you for a while now. You're a great surgeon, but after the Woods case you started fracturing yourself. Your duties never suffered, so I left it alone. I ignored it. I had hoped that you would be able to deal with it and move on. In a way you're still dealing with it. I know you married that woman just so she could have the benefits."

"George..."

George held up his hand to cut Oliver off. "No, I'm not done."

Oliver closed his mouth and sat back. It was time for him to just accept it. After all, if he just stalled by letting George talk, then he'd be able to find another way or give Josh the time he needed. "Very well."

"Whatever the two of you have going on, is between the two of you. If she's using you for benefits, that's fine because that's between the two of you. I think it's a bunch of horse hockey, but that's your business, not mine. You've grown up a lot. I think you're even beginning to become a good man. I already know you're a great surgeon. You're playing with the rules — the rules that are there for a reason."

"George, I love her. I love them both. I'm just trying to do what I need to do to get Dani cared for. That's all."

"That's all good and fine. However,..." He took a pause and Oliver knew, knew it was time for him to accept his punishment. "You crossed a line, Oliver. It's a line I can't ignore." George shook his head, his shoulders hunched slightly. "Oliver, you signed a contract. That contract is very explicit. You can't work another job during hours that you're on our payroll. I know you didn't have any surgeries during that time, but that's time that we paid you and you weren't here."

"I was available though."

"I'm aware of that. That's why I let this go on for so long."

Ollie flinched from shock. Had George known? "What do you mean?"

"Quit acting like a dumb twit. I've known since you signed the papers on the building. I'm not an idiot."

"I never said you were."

"You're a terrible liar, but it's true that you've never underestimated me. You've just overestimated yourself... You should really be more careful with your phone."

Oliver frowned for a moment before recognition flared to life. The day he signed the papers, he was late because he lost his phone. His un-protected, no password having phone... it had fallen out of his lab coat, yet he had found it on his desk... "How?"

"Master key, moron." The hurtful words were smoothed with the smile George aimed his way. "Oliver, you have to understand that I'm stuck. I need something to be able to fix this, but right now my hands are tied behind my back. The board has asked that you be suspended, pending action. They voted. They're calling for a peer review on all of your cases since Woods."

They were ending his career in medicine. "George, that's not necessary."

"It's either that or you resign. If you resign it stays quiet and you might still be able to practice." George scrubbed his face, as if trying to rub the stress away. "I don't like this, but the board… they're not pleased."

"What can I do to change their minds?"

George gave a half-hearted laugh. "Buy control of the hospital," he suggested.

A frantic, heavy-handed knock on the door interrupted Oliver's retort. The door flew open and a tiny woman stalked in. She was about seventy-nine years old. Her face was contorted in an angry manner and her whitish-blue hair stood at odd angles. "You won't believe this! Some asshole bought control of my hospital! Our investors weren't paying attention and they sold fifty-one percent of our stock."

"Really?"

Oliver watched as George tried to hid a smile. He watched as the tension seemed to melt away from George and the lines on his face smoothed out.

"Yes! Three corporations bought stock this morning. All under one head corporation, Hunt Enterprises."

Hunt Enterprises? Oliver squirmed in his seat. He knew who owned Hunt Enterprises.

"I don't understand it either! They're a technology and real estate company. Why would they want our hospital? Are they going to close us down? Build something else here? The Board is gong nuts! As CEO I need to be able to reassure them that everything's ok, but I can't do that! Why can't I do that, you ask? Because I don't know that it will be!" She stalked back and forth, pacing in the tiny room. Whisps of hair flew about her face.

"Beth, I'd like to introduce someone to you." George motioned to Oliver. "Beth, this is Oliver Brooks. His father owns Hunt Enterprises."

The woman turned to Oliver and gave him such a look of distain that he felt as if he had been tossed into a supernova. "Why does he want our company?"

"I don't know." Oliver shrugged. He really didn't know. There was no reason for his father to care about Avalon.

"Yes, you do. I bet you're here to scout it out for him!" She pointed a bony finger at him. "I bet he's been planning this for months and he sent you to see what we'd do."

George stood up and sighed deeply. "No, Beth. Actually, Dr. Brooks is the neurosurgeon that the board requested a resignation for this morning. You remember, that vote you were leading. The one I told you was a bad idea. I'm pretty sure his father got word of it shortly after and took action. His father is a very wealthy man after all."

Why would his father buy the hospital? Was it because of their argument?

"I don't give a damn how wealthy his father is! This is absurd!"

"George?" Oliver wasn't sure what to do. This elderly woman was throwing a temper tantrum. He had never seen anything like it. "Should I leave?"

"Stay where you are." George commanded before turning back to the woman. "Beth, Dr. Brooks has been an extremely valuable asset to this hospital, however, he holds no key functions that would prevent his father from buying the hospital. As a matter of fact, we could use this to our advantage. Beth, have you thought about advertising the fact that our top neurosurgeon runs a free clinic in his limited spare time?"

"It's improper and against his contract!"

"Beth, what's the big deal? Sure, we use contracts to protect our patients, but he didn't harm any patients. He was trying to help. We all took the Hippocratic Oath. I think you need to start thinking long term. Sure, you can fire Dr. Brooks, if that makes you feel better, but let's think about the clinic. If we used this to our advantage... it would go over very well with the public, don't you think?"

Beth glared at George.

George sat calmly.

It was a poker match and Oliver knew he didn't have any cards in the game. If only he could just disappear from the room. If only he could pretend he was never there.

The silence was deafening.

Beth turned to Oliver and his wish to disappear grew. "Fine. We'll need to clean you up, but it might work. George, make him presentable. If his father is going to take over my hospital then I'm going to take over his free clinic." She glared at Oliver. "Be prepared to work your ass off, young man. You're not going to get off easy."

Chapter 21

OLLIE ENTERED DANI'S ROOM WHERE Synthia was waiting for him. "Ollie, they found a donor! It's a match! They're going to save her!" Tears streamed down her face as she launched herself at him.

As he caught her, wrapping his arms around her and pulling her tightly to him, he knew that he wanted to be with her. She was his wife and he loved her.

"That's wonderful!" He had been told the same thing over the phone, but knew that she just needed to tell him herself.

She pulled back and kissed him.

It was a deep, sensual kiss that he lost himself in until a knock on the door interrupted them. Pulling back from her, he looked toward the door. There, stood his father.

Ollie lowered Synthia to the ground. "Synthia, I'm going to need to handle this. Where are the papers that I need to sign?"

"I signed them for you." He looked at her, impressed. "What? You married me to save my daughter, the least I could do was forge your signature while the guy was yelling at you."

"You knew where I was?"

"Yeah, George told me that he was going to have to talk

to you about closing down the clinic. He said it would make you really upset… Ollie, he told me about Lucy."

Lucy. George had told Synthia about Lucy. His mind raced, his heart thumped in a steady race to explode a valve, and his left eye began twitching.

"Ollie, it's ok. Go with your dad. We'll talk later."

"Lucy…"

"Ollie, go talk to your father."

She was right. He needed to try to set things right. Maybe his father hadn't given up on him, maybe his father had been in his corner the only way the man knew how to be there. It was time to put the past to rest — time to be the man that he knew his mother wanted him to be.

"Dad, you look like you could use a cup of coffee."

His father startled at his words like he was expecting more anger, more frustration. Ollie was tired of being angry. Coffee was all he could offer up at the moment. Coffee and crow.

☾

Ollie sat across the table from his father, silently staring at him. His eyes looked tired, but his jaw was set. Ollie smiled. His father thought he didn't know. "So? How are things with you?" It was a simple question. Simple questions were safe questions.

"Good. How are things with you?" His father stirred the coffee sitting in front of him, black with two sugars. Ollie doubted his father had ever even looked at a latte or a frappachino.

"Some mysterious company bought the hospital, so I got to keep my job." *Keep it casual*, he reminded himself.

"Oh, good. I know you like working there."

"Dad, can we cut the crap?" Ollie's voice sounded tired

to him and he vaguely wondered what it sounded like to his father.

The surprised and unsettled look his father gave him made him realize just what all he had missed by not paying attention — by being selfish. "I'm serious. Talk to me."

"Ok, what do you want to talk about?"

"Dad, I wanna know why — why you left me alone?"

"Are you talking about boarding school?" Ollie nodded. "I didn't know what to do with you… you were just a kid and my wife just died." He father sighed and pushed his coffee away. "I know it was shitty, but I honestly didn't know what to do. Your mom, she was the love of my life. She and I were supposed to be together until we were both old and gray. Then we were supposed to die together."

"You haven't even dated since she died, have you?"

"Nope. It feels like cheating." His father reached for the coffee. Holding it like it could warm his soul before taking a sip. Sitting it back down, he went back to stirring it aimlessly.

"Ollie, the boarding school seemed like a good idea at the time. I had things to go through and do. Boxing up her things… it was one of the worst things I've ever had to do. I didn't want you to be hurt anymore and you looked so much like her."

His father seemed broken. For the first time, Ollie was realizing that what Synthia had said was true. Drake Brooks had lost the love of his life and had been broken. Drake Brooks had no idea what to do when he lost the one person that meant the world to him. He did the only thing he could, push away the son that reminded him of his deceased wife.

" Son, it was so painful… You still remind me so much of her, but it doesn't hurt anymore. It hasn't for years —

since you were about seven. However, I didn't know how to fix things with you. I just hoped that you would forgive me at some point without me ever having to ask."

That was the most his father had said to him in years. Ollie was speechless. How did he respond to his father's admission? How could he respond? The man had finally opened up to him after years of silence, years of anguish.

"Dad…"

"No, I need you to understand… I never knew how to tell you what I was going through. I never knew how to tell you that you have your mother's smile, her eyes, her humor, her intellect. I never knew how to tell you that when you laugh it reminds me of how much I missed her — how much I still do."

Tears. His father was crying.

"Ollie, I need you to know this because I'm tired of you shutting me out of your life. I've put up with it because you're simply returning the favor, but I need it to stop. I'm an old man now. I want to be part of your life. I might not deserve it, but I want it."

"Dad, stop."

"No, you need to know… I love you, Ollie. I love you and you're my son. There's never been a moment that I didn't love you. There's never been a moment that I wasn't thinking of you."

Ollie thought about it and realized that while Frank had always been the one to ask him questions about what was going on in his life the answers had always gotten back to his father. His father had always known, one way or another, what was important to Ollie.

"Dad, I know you saved my job by buying the hospital."

Startled, his father knocked over his coffee. Grabbing a napkin and mopping it up as quickly as he could, Ollie berated himself. He should have approached it more gently than that.

"How could you know?"

"Who else would buy the hospital to keep me from getting fired?"

His father's mouth opened and closed several times, reminding Ollie of a fish.

"What? Did you think it could be any number of people that were just waiting to bail me out?"

"Well, it could have been…"

"Get real. Only six people would have enough cash to do that and only two would be willing. Jack didn't think about it, so that leaves you."

His father turned away from him and looked out, surveying the cafeteria. They had wasted so much time. "Dad, I need a favor."

"Yes?"

"Dani has a donor set up."

"That's wonderful!"

"It is, but we're going to need some help. Avalon's CEO has decided that I'm going to be pulling double duty for a while, I want Synthia to go back to school… did you know she was studying to be a physicist before Dani was born?"

"No, that's wonderful. I always knew you would find a smart woman."

"Yeah, but with Dani needing so much care I don't think she'll want to leave her with just anyone."

"I might be able to find someone to help you guys."

"I was thinking that maybe you could help. Maybe you could sit with Dani for a few days a week while we work on getting Synthia through school. She deserves it. She's put her life on hold for far too long… I want her to have something to remember me by."

"You love her."

It was a statement, a declaration, and it was true. Ollie loved her. It had swept him up in a storm that he'd never seen coming. His stomach was in knots and his heart hurt at the thought of her leaving him.

"Are you going to tell her?"

"After Dani's transplant. I don't want to distract her."

"Son, love isn't a distraction. Love is powerful and full of possibilities. It can give you the ability to do amazing things, things you'd never do otherwise. You need to tell her and you need to do it soon."

Ollie frowned. Had he been mistaken at thinking she needed to focus on Dani? Or was his father right? Would she feel the same or would she run away as quickly as she could?

Everything could go right, or it could go wrong. Love was strange and painful. Could he risk telling Synthia?

Chapter 22

SITTING IN THE WAITING ROOM was the worst thing. Patients came and went, time seemed to slow to the speed of molasses, and questions playing over in his mind never ceased. He had never imagined what the wait was like for his patient's families, but now he knew. Now he knew how terrible it was to wait for word on a loved one.

"Ollie, I know this isn't the time… I need to tell you something…"

Oliver looked at Synthia. She was so beautiful and she was his wife. "Everything's going to be ok. They'll come any minute to tell us that she's doing great."

"No, that's not it. I'm not worried about that." She wrung her hands nervously. Her tone was shy. "Ollie, I love you."

She loved him.

"Why?"

"What?"

"Why do you love me?" It was hard to believe that she did.

"Do I really need a reason?" She grinned at him. He nodded at her. "Ollie, I love you because you're Ollie. Dani and I haven't found any one that measured up to what we needed until you came in the picture. You married me to save my daughter."

"So you love me because I helped you…" The thought was depressing. That wasn't love, just convenience.

"For a neurosurgeon you're awfully ridiculous." She took a deep breath and blew it slowly out. "You've been there for us and never asked for anything in return. You were there and that's what mattered. You haven't let me down once, and the sex was great."

A laugh escaped him. She loved him because the sex was great.

"Ollie, I'm serious. I love you because you're you. You're smart, loving, and kind. You look at me with wonder and treat Dani like she's yours. You have to know what that does to a woman."

Looking at Synthia, Ollie realized that he wished what she was saying was true. He wished that she really loved him, that she loved him for no reason other than he was Oliver. Not Dr. Oliver Brooks. Just Oliver. "Everything is going to be ok."

"Oliver," the nurse called.

"Yes?"

"The donor just woke up. He was asking to speak to you."

What? That was against policy. The donor shouldn't know the recipient or their family. "How did he find out my name?"

"I'm not supposed to say anything, but Dr. Montoya…"

The jerk. He told the donor that it was for a doctor's daughter. That's how come the donor was willing to do it…

"Dr. Montoya told him because of who he is… I just thought you should know… I know how much it tore you up."

"Who is the donor?"

"Mr. Woods."

He froze. Was it the same person? Was it really Lucy Woods' father?

"He's in the Recovery Room and would like to speak to you."

☾

"Hi, Doc."

"Hi, Mr. Woods." Oliver shuffled his feet. Why was he here? What could this man possibly want from him?

"I just wanted to apologize."

Apologize? For what? Oliver was the one that killed his daughter.

"I know you're probably pretty surprised at this. I registered as a donor after Luce died. I had a really hard time with that and I took it out on you. You couldn't have known about the clot. I'm sorry for how I acted. I shouldn't have blamed you."

The clot was there. It was plain as day. Sure, it hadn't shown up on the scans, but that didn't mean that Oliver shouldn't have expected it. "Mr. Woods, I…"

"No. Please let me finish?"

Oliver nodded.

"The Registry gave Enrique my information, so he could determine if I was a match. That man has never broken a law in his entire life… except for me. He told me who the patient was. You might not have been able to save my daughter, but I could save yours."

Montoya? He broke HIPAA? The man that would follow the rulebook even if it told him to jump off a bridge? "I don't understand…"

"Enrique isn't a bad guy. He just hasn't had an easy life.

My father helped bring him to the States when he was just a baby… My father lied to keep him here… I know you'll understand the predicament he was in. He knew I was your daughter's only hope. I know that right now you're having a hard time understanding this, but I hope one day you'll be able to understand."

"Understand what?"

"Understand that, Enrique just gave up his career, so that I could apologize to you."

Apologize? What did he have to apologize for? Oliver was the one that took his daughter from him. Oliver was the one that didn't… couldn't save Lucy.

"I've followed everything you've done since. You're a good man, but you took Luce's death to heart. That was my fault. It was her time to go. Sure, I miss her every single day, but it was her time. You gave me more time with her, until there wasn't any way to make more time. Enrique looked over her file for me. He said without you treating her, she would have died six months sooner. You gave me six months extra with my baby. You're not God, but you did something that would have been impossible for anyone else."

Was it true? Had he really given him an extra six months with his daughter?

"I just hope that I can give you more time with your daughter. Make the most of it while you can."

"Why are you doing this for me?"

"Because you gave me enough time with Luce for her to do something amazing. She knew she was dying. She knew the surgery wouldn't work."

"How do you know that?"

"She left me something… Notes To Her Dad, she called it. The simplest thing in the world to some, but to me… It's a guide to live by. She was over the moon that we

were able to go see things and do things before she died...
It meant more than anything to her... I just wanted to
return the favor to you. To give you more time, just like
you gave to Luce. It's all I can do."

Oliver scrubbed at the tears trailing down his cheeks.
Lucy had mentioned to him that she was writing letters
to her dad just in case the surgery didn't work, but he
didn't think much of it. Instead he had been the stereo-
typical detached surgeon... He had done doctor speak
and ignored something that was so important to her.

"I think it's time you reviewed her case file, from new
eyes. Sit with Enrique and let him show you what you
haven't been able to see — what grief's clouded you from.
Now, go be with your wife and daughter. She should be
waking up soon."

Chapter 23

SYNTHIA STOOD SILENTLY IN FRONT of the door to the recovery room. The door seemed to be too much for her like its weight was greater than anything she could move. Oliver sighed deeply. It was time for him to choose.

Choice. It was a terrible thing because you never knew if you were making the right choice or not. You just had to pick one on the best information that you had at hand.

Ollie had a choice to make. He had to either let go of the past and move on or give it all up. His job at the hospital was now safe, thanks to his father. The only question left was, was his relationship with Synthia going to perish or thrive? It was his choice.

Holding his head high, he stepped up beside her. "I'm not perfect. I make mistakes."

They both looked forward through the tiny window at Dani. Her pale form made his stomach lurch. She was prone, still sleeping, but was alive. Relief stole over him. She was alive. He felt Synthia's hand take his and give it a little squeeze.

Taking a deep breath he made his choice. "I promise I will do whatever it takes to protect you both. I don't know how it happened, but somehow along the way, I fell in love with you. I hate that I don't know how it happened and I can't tell you the exact moment when. I wish I could, but I think it was something to do with how you fought for Dani no matter what. How you still argued with everyone and knew what was best for her. How you sought what was best for her."

Oliver felt like telling her what she meant to him was just too much. It was stripping him emotionally bare. She had to understand. She had to know that his heart was being ravaged by emotion, his mind was being ripped apart trying to figure out the right words to say what he felt.

He couldn't turn to look at her. It was too much. It was time to tell her about Lucy.

"Synthia, there's something you should know... the clinic... I started it because of Lucy." The words hurt, but it was time they were said. "She was a little girl that loved unicorns. I was her surgeon, removing a tumor that was... It was a terribly complicated surgery. There was a blood clot that didn't show on any of the scans. It was right below the tumor..."

Her sharp intake of breath made him pause to gather his thoughts. He had never talked about Lucy and the day his life changed.

"Synthia, the blood clot... we couldn't stop it. I tried. We gave her blood while we tried to stop it. We did everything we could. It wasn't enough. Lucy died. I had to tell her father that she was gone. I didn't want to ever have to do that again, but it was inevitable. I opened the clinic to give back. I was punishing myself. I just needed to make amends. I never thought that something so great would come out of something so terrible."

He squeezed her hand again. "You and Dani, you guys are the best thing in my life. I don't want to lose you."

"Ollie, I think there's something you should know…"

He froze, she was about to tell him how much she despised him, that she did it for the benefits, or even that she loved someone else… She was about to tell him that she really didn't love him, that said it because she was frightened…

"Ollie, I fell for you the minute you sat on the hospital bed with Daniella and told her that sometimes parents fight. I never knew she heard us, but you knew just what to say to her. I was frozen with terror at all the things she must have heard, but you stepped right up. You plowed through the hard discussions. You were a rock… I can't ever not love you for that."

Oliver frowned. "What does that mean?"

"I would like for you to go in here with me. Then I would like for you to take me home and make love to me. I would like to share your bed every night from now on, for the rest of eternity. I love you."

"Because I was there for you?"

"No, because you're Oliver Brooks you dummy."

"The neurosurgeon…"

"No, you're Oliver Brooks, the man that loves me because I'm me and the man that I love because he's him. You're not a neurosurgeon to me. You're not a wealthy man. You're simply a man that is generous, kind, and treats me with the love that I deserve. You're a man that loves my daughter and was willing to do whatever was necessary for her."

Oliver felt relief at her words. He squeezed her hand back. "When we get home, I'm going to do more than kiss you."

"I can't wait. You're such a tease, I've been dying."

He turned to her and saw that she grinned at him. The grin on her face told him that she was already anticipating it.

Everything was going to be fine. They were going to be fine.

Chapter 24

SYNTHIA STOOD AT THE DOORFRAME waiting to be called in the church. She took a breath and smoothed down the front of her silk white dress, admiring how pretty it was.

Ollie had given her everything. She lightly caressed her stomach and smiled. He had given her more than she ever dreamed possible.

"Will you tell him tonight?"

Her head snapped up at Ollie's dad's voice. "Hn? Tell him what?"

"That you're pregnant. You should tell him tonight. You're already married, this is just for me. Well, sort of for me. I always wanted a daughter. When my wife died I thought I'd never get one. Then when Frank called me and told me about how Ollie was marrying you, I was over the moon with joy. I knew it wouldn't be long. Now, if it's a girl I hope you'll consider the name Tabitha, after Ollie's mom. If it's a boy then I hope you'll consider Jacques Cousteau."

"The famous explorer?"

"Of course! He was the whole reason Ollie went to medical school. Kid thought I didn't know that he was obsessed with that scientist, just because I had him in boarding school. He should know better. I'm his father and I will always be involved in his life."

"I'm glad that you and Ollie got everything aired out. I wish my own father could be here to walk me down the aisle, but you're the next best thing." Thinking about her father, the tears threatened to fall again. He had passed away within hours of learning that she had gotten married.

She caressed her stomach again. She never got to tell him that he had another grandchild on the way or that she loved Ollie. She smiled, he knew that she would be ok. He never would have gone in his sleep if he hadn't. He was the kind of man that would have told the grim reaper he'd need to come back at another time, whether it worked or not.

"Come along then. Let's get you to your husband before he thinks you've run away with someone." Drake winked at her. They both knew Ollie was more worried about the wedding than anyone else. The man had planned every detail with Jack. Synthia had only needed to choose colors and cake.

Her stomach rumbled at thinking of the cake. It was delicious.

"I'll tell him tonight, but I think he may have already suspected."

"Why do you say that?"

"I caught him looking at baby websites. At the time I thought he was thinking about switching fields. Then last night I began to wonder if he knew the truth all along."

"Ollie always knows the truth, even if he doesn't want to know it. It just takes him some time to realize it."

Synthia slipped her arm in his and they turned to walk through the door. "I think he's going to be a terrific father."

"He sure will. He's already learned what not to do." As he winked at her, the music began to play.

The room was filled with loved ones, family members and friends from both sides. All were rooting for them, hoping that they had a fantastic day and life full of love and happiness. She saw Jack and his current fling, a guy named Bob. She saw Enrique Montoya and Mr. Woods. She also saw her friends from what felt like her previous life. Willy and Sheila both stood there proudly, smiling at her.

She was so happy. Her daughter was there, alive and well, tossing flowers on the carpet in front of her.

It was hard to top this moment.

As they stopped next to Ollie, his father kissed her cheek and walked away. She turned to Ollie and saw that he was emotional at seeing her. "Hi, hon. I missed you."

He nodded, but seemed unable to speak.

"While I have you here, I have a surprise for you. I'm pregnant."

He nodded once again, but didn't speak.

"Ollie?"

Once again he nodded, as tears slipped down his cheeks. "I know," he croaked out. "I'm going to be a dad." He wrapped his arms around her, and kissed her cheek. "I'm going to be a dad."

"Yes, and you're going to be a fantastic one. You know how I know this?"

"How?"

"Because you already are a fantastic one to Dani." She lightly caressed his cheek. "Now, Oliver Brooks, are you going to marry me again or do we need another shotgun wedding?"

He laughed at her joke and wiped his tears away before wiping away her own. "Of course I'll marry you. I already did, didn't I?"

"Then let's get to it. Where's Frank? Frank?"

"I'm right here. We were just giving you two a moment. Are we ready to start?"

"Yes," they both shouted in unison. The entire congregation giggled in response.

"Very well, let's get this party on the road."

The End

About Brina

You can find out about Brina and follow her on
Facebook:
www.facebook.com/brina99cary/?fref=ts